Ask Again Later

Also by JILL A. DAVIS

Girls' Poker Night

Ask Again

ecce

An Imprint of HarperCollins*Publishers*

Jill A. Davis

—

Ask Again Later

HarperCollins books may be purchased for educational,
business, or sales promotional use. For information, please
write: Special Markets Department, HarperCollins
Publishers, 10 East 53rd Street, New York, NY 10022.

FIRST EDITION

Designed by Barbara M. Bachman

LIBRARY OF CONGRESS CATALOGING-IN-PUBLICATION DATA
IS AVAILABLE UPON REQUEST.

ISBN-10: 0-06-087596-8
ISBN: 978-0-06-087596-1

07 08 09 10 11 WBC/RRD 10 9 8 7 6 5 4 3 2

With love,
For Ed and Campbell

Missed Opportunities

I CAN REMEMBER the first Christmas after my father left. I was five. We didn't get a tree that year. We didn't buy gifts. Somehow it seemed pathetic to deck the halls and all—when Dad wasn't there. We missed opportunities. And I got really good at missing opportunities.

I am Emily. Emily Rhode. When I was in second grade, I experimented with changing my identity by misspelling my last name. I had hopes that a new spelling might transform me and permit me access to a new home, and a new life.

Sometimes it was Road. Or Rowed, and even Rode. Almost no one ever noticed the way my name was spelled. People just assume you're going to get your own name right. Except for Miss Bryan, my English teacher. She seemed curious. Or, at the very least, not comatose. She gave us an assignment.

"Write one paragraph about your home," said Miss Bryan. "Spelling counts."

Write about home . . . should I tell her the combination

to the safe, too? I was eager to share, the perfect accomplice, and I didn't need more than one sentence. The sentence is as true today as it was twenty years ago: Home is a place you can never leave behind. I liked that it was both insistent and ambiguous. I spelled my name correctly, because spelling counts.

While you can't leave it behind, you can look at the events of your past from a new point of view. Turn them around. See all the angles. Consider it your second chance. Second chances do come your way. Like trains, they arrive and depart regularly. Recognizing the ones that matter is the trick.

Plexiglas

MY OFFICE CHAIR IS parked behind a small desk, and on the desk is a giant phone. I intentionally use the word *parked* because the chair is enormous and—if you believe the old wives' tales—engineered by the Ford Motor Company.

In front of my desk is an impressive wall of bulletproof Plexiglas. It's the one thing I'll miss about this crappy job when I leave. I've been able to work in confidence knowing that if someone tries to shoot me—the fabulously sultry gal who answers the telephone—the bullets will bounce mockingly off of the Plexiglas and not disturb me from the important business of answering the telephone.

When the phone doesn't ring for a while, I start to

think about bringing in my own gun and taking a couple of shots at the Plexiglas to test it. Sure the manufacturer *says* it's bulletproof. I don't own a piece though, and when I call a shooting range somewhere in Millbrook, New York, they tell me not to call again. Ever. They refused to answer my question. How much will it cost to hire a guy to take a couple of shots at a piece of Plexiglas in a Midtown high-rise? It isn't their line of work, they claim.

"Yeah, but bottom line it for me, sister. Send a body out to gimme an estimate. Bottom line it for me," I say.

"You're crazy, lady," they say, and hang up. I'm just killing time and hoping they'll play along, and I'm disappointed when they refuse. For a moment I worry that I work for one of those companies that monitors its phone calls under the guise of quality control. I am instantly comforted when I realize I work for a law firm too disorganized to tap its own phones.

To say all I do is answer phones is to seriously downplay my role around here. I also control the buzzer button that opens the main door, allowing lawyers into their offices after they get off of the elevator, or return from the bathroom.

Sometimes I fail to push the buzzer with the deftness they might like. I eat up a second of this person's life, five seconds of that person's life. The ones who grow impatient quickly and who are easily angered are the ones I steal twenty seconds from for the sheer pleasure of it. They grunt and growl in sincere pissiness, and it makes me feel terrific, alive in that way that you don't feel often enough.

Propaganda

I DAYDREAM—AND GET paid for it. I recall a scene from *An Officer and a Gentleman*. At the end of the movie Richard Gere, dressed in his naval whites, goes into a factory, picks up Debra Winger, and carries her out of that depressing place with all of those dirty machines.

I wish that would happen to me. Of course the whole time I'd be worried that the guy was trying to guess my weight or something. I realize how truly pathetic I am. Some guy in a uniform drags his woman out of the workplace to stick her in a house to cook and possibly even clip coupons, and I am starting to buy into it, into the anti-female propaganda disguised as romance. As soon as he picks her up, things have to head south from there, because at some point, he has to put her down.

I blame my father for my current situation. It's so much easier to blame him than rehash my past and actually work through it. Instead, I pin all of my disappointment and loss on my current post. I can't decide what's worse, clock-watching or minimum wage. Luckily, I'm steeped in both, so I don't have to choose.

The world of nepotism is ugly and dark. I know. There are people out there paying their dues who probably deserve to sit behind this Plexiglas more than I do. If not for the fact that my father is so well connected, I'd be forced to do a job I got solely on merit. I'd be working as a lawyer, on track to make partner, at a firm where a senior partner was not 50 percent responsible for creating me. I would be boosting my résumé and sleeping with young enthusiasts of all things legal. The notion of being shot would, in all likelihood, not even occur to me. It certainly wouldn't preoccupy me. I may be the only professional in history to take several giant steps backward by cashing in on my "connections."

Habits

I INHALE A DRAG from an imaginary cigarette being held in an imaginary cigarette holder, recline in my massive chair, and say to nobody, "Jesus is coming . . . and I haven't a thing to wear." I say this as if I were preparing to attend one of those cocktail parties at which the women wear giant fake pearls and have the alcohol tolerance of a four-hundred-pound man. I go to great lengths to amuse myself because, you see, no one else does.

I'm one of those people who other people like but never remember. I think most of the world is probably like me. Until recently nothing about me was outstanding, and then my mother got cancer. It's a disease people like to talk about, so I'm more popular now. And when I flip through magazines, I read the breast cancer articles first, even before the numerology column.

At lunchtime I walk downstairs to the lobby and buy

the tallest, thickest magazines I can find, then walk down Fifth Avenue with them propped up in front of my chest. I've grown to feel naked without the Plexiglas shield.

If a sniper tried to get me, would the magazines stop the bullets? I had great confidence that *Vogue,* particularly their September issue, might have the heft to stop a shower of hot lead. A cautious person by nature, I skip every few steps, hop on one foot, turn around, duck down, and pop up. If a sniper is waiting for me, watching me, well, he is going to work for this hit. I am no one's easy mark.

The woman who waters the plants at the law firm sees me and steps up her pace heading in the other direction. I want to call out to her to explain, but she waters plants for a living. What would she know of dodging bullets? Of the loveliness of a squinted eye pressed tight against the cool scope of a rifle? If you've got dead leaves, root rot, she's your gal. Of course maybe she's being warehoused, too. Her greatness ripening right there on the branch of life that is the weighted, muggy air of Midtown.

Free Ride

MY FATHER AND I commute to the office together. I walk from York to Fifth and meet him on the corner of Seventy-ninth.

Today he has a shopping bag, which he clumsily presents to me.

"It's for you," Jim says.

He hails a cab. In the backseat of the car, I open the box that's inside of the bag. There is a suit for me. Gray flannel with chalk-colored pinstripes.

"Thanks," I say. Then I notice that it matches his suit. The words *Dad* and *Lad* come to mind.

"Wow. You really wanted a son, didn't you?" I say.

"No, sir! Why would you say that?" Jim says, pointing out that it's a skirt and jacket, not pants and jacket.

"You just called me 'sir' . . ." I say.

"Buster, I call everyone sir," Jim says.

"Thank you," I say. I think it's the only gift I've ever received from him that he selected himself. "Seriously, thanks."

"You're welcome," Jim says. "You don't have to wear it if you don't want to. What you're wearing is just fine."

It's bittersweet, of course. He thinks he gets a say in what I wear. The subconscious owns no fancy timepiece. In his mind there's been no gap. Nothing lost. I'm still five.

Pizza Party

WENDY, THE OFFICE MANAGER, approaches me with papers in hand. "It's Sarah's birthday today; want to sign her card?" Wendy asks. "She's going to be—oh, I'll never tell!" She laughs, and smiles. "Okay, forty-two. She's going to be forty-two. But you didn't hear that from me!"

"I don't know who Sarah is," I say. "Do you still want me to sign the card?"

"Sarah's really nice. You'll like her. She works in billing. She's been here forever. We're getting pizza and cake. Party starts at six in the conference room," Wendy says.

"Okay," I say. I sign the card. "Dear Sarah, Happy Birthday. I look forward to meeting you. —Emily"

"Okay, now I just need four dollars for the pizza and cake. Everyone chips in," Wendy says, "fair and square."

"Oh, okay," I say. "I don't have change for a five. Keep the dollar."

"No, no, I'll bring your change back to you," Wendy says. "This is strictly nonprofit."

She puts a checkmark next to my name and makes a note that she owes me a dollar.

I look at the employee list. There are thirteen professionals and eight support staff, including myself. Twenty people (not including the birthday girl), each contributing four dollars. Eighty dollars for pizza and cake.

I buzz extension #1.

"Hello?" Jim says.

Jim is so many things. He is my boss. He is my father. He is where I place the blame for my incomplete and unsatisfactory relationships with men.

"I think you should start paying for pizza and cake for staff parties," I say.

"Okay," Jim says.

In general, he's so much more agreeable than I ever could have imagined.

"Don't you want to know why?" I ask.

"Sure—why?" Jim asks.

"Someone's wasting ninety minutes getting a birth-day card signed, collecting cash from people, making change, interrupting those who are working . . . it's more cost-effective for the firm to pay for the party. She doesn't even carry change with her—just to prolong the process," I say.

Silence.

"Well," Jim says, "I get the impression Wendy likes arranging these festivities. I agree that the process is a waste of time. But it does give her a real sense of getting out of work. Being paid to chat people up. I think it's a good outlet for her."

"Well, then, never mind," I say. "But why not give her a raise if you want her to be satisfied and excited about her job?"

"Oh, I think she's happy with her salary. It's the work she's not so fond of," Jim says. "I think everyone in this office can relate to that, don't you?"

"Yeah," I say.

Secret Life

I LISTEN IN on my father's personal phone conversa-tions through the firm's not-so-sophisticated phone sys-tem. Mostly boring stuff. Sometimes he's very funny, but I can't quite figure out if it's because he has a highly devel-oped sense of humor or if it's because he's out of touch.

I secretly need to know him, and spying on him seems like good practice for not missing opportunities. If he knew I was listening to his calls, I don't think he'd care, which makes this breach of trust easy to justify and too tempting to ignore.

I make a list of his best traits. Traits that are less obvious outside of work. At work, he's competent. Smart. Nice. Caring. Generous. Outside of work, he's lost. The one place left that is safe for us to go is work.

At approximately eight thirty-five each morning, while reading the *New York Post,* he calls officer manager Wendy Corbett's extension. She's always in the staff kitchen making the second pot of coffee at that time. So curious was I that I finally got the courage to listen in on the daily call. Turns out he leaves each day's horoscope for Aries on her voice mail. Last week it was Valentine's Day, and he left two messages. Her horoscope and her romance-scope.

Yesterday I heard him talking to a woman, in a whisper that was supposed to sound sexy or something. I suspended my own private wiretap for the rest of the afternoon out of empathetic embarrassment. Today there have been a series of calls from a younger woman.

We all regress when we're scared. Why shouldn't he? That was his upside to our crisis. During my mother's treatments he started a maniacal dating spree. It has always been his favorite coping mechanism. A similar spree ended my parents' marriage twenty-five years ago.

A few weeks ago he was dating a woman who'd graduated from school three years ahead of me and made her living selling makeup out of a pink suitcase. When she was in the waiting room, I was curious, so I asked to hear her sales pitch and ended up buying some moderately priced lip gloss from her out of guilt. We chatted for twenty minutes. There was nothing overtly objectionable about her, and at the same time there was nothing obviously wonderful either. Yet my father landed himself here.

There are moments when I believe I could travel down this path of thought and never return. But the ringing phone snatches me back—a literal tether to reality.

Breakdown

IF I WERE LOOKING at a map of my life, this is the point of the journey at which I'd have to ask myself: How the hell did I end up *here*? Answering phones? Reunited with my father? Trying to micromanage office pizza parties? This was not the future I envisioned. These are not the dreams I hatched while sleeping on rainbow sheets in my single bed. It has nothing to do with lack of ambition. Far from it. I graduated from college and went directly to law school without taking a summer break. Two days after graduating from law school I started logging seventy-hour workweeks at the respected firm of Schroeder, Sotos, Willett, and Ritchie.

I kept myself buried in work. Obsessed with it. Glancing up every so often to see there were other important things in the world. Things I had no time for until my mother found a lump. A small lump that changed everything.

All of the things in my life that worked suddenly seemed broken. So I abandoned my former life. Truth be told? It was an emergency escape hatch that released me from a job that had kidnapped my personal life, and got me out of a relationship I was too afraid to engage in.

When pressed to tell people how I got myself into my current nepotism-gone-bad situation, I like to describe it as a mini-breakdown. The prefix makes all the difference. It makes it sound more like a vacation than a condition best treated with medication and art therapy.

I can pinpoint the morning that things changed. As usual, I was on a self-improvement mission from the time the alarm clock sounded. Each morning I woke with the same promise to myself. I would work less and live more. Every day I broke that promise and ate takeout for dinner at my desk and pretended not to be in love with Sam. I was looking for ways to enhance my life without having to change anything significant.

My Shrink

PAUL'S OFFICE IS COZY, and by cozy I mean there is a white wicker daybed in lieu of a couch. The first time I came to see him there were pastel-colored butterfly sheets on the daybed, and I almost didn't come back because of that single detail. I tortured myself with what it could all mean—his choice in sheets. Are we all meant to soar in this world? To see things from the vantage point of a metamorphosing insect? Or were they just sheets that happened to fit the daybed? As soon as he gets an actual couch, I'll be lying on it. Until then, I'll sit across from him in the black, foam-stuffed pleather club chair.

"So, what's happening in your internal life?" Paul asks.

"Who's got time for an internal life?" I say.

"Not a hell of a lot happening in your conscious life," Paul says.

"Ouch," I say.

"Well, not anything you're willing to talk about," Paul says.

I steal a glance at him. He needs a haircut. Like all shrinks, he wants me to talk about my mother.

"Whatever happened to that guy? The one who had the appointment after me?" I ask.

"Why do you ask?" Paul says.

"I think I miss him," I say. I can't handle separations that aren't accompanied by lots of advance notice.

"I see," Paul says.

"You cured him, and I'm not sure I'll be able to forgive you," I say.

Silence.

"Because you miss him? Or because I 'cured' him and not you?" Paul asks.

I look him over for thirty seconds or so.

"You're good! And feisty, too," I say. "But either way you're in the wrong, and I'm not forgiving you."

He laughs. His eyes go from happy to sad on a dime. A hair trigger. He's mastered empathy.

"I liked that ratty backpack he carried. Even though he was too old to carry a backpack—in my opinion. And then, just before he stopped seeing you, he switched to a leather briefcase. No scuffs. Brand new. I should have taken that as a sign," I say.

"Sign of what?" Paul asks.

"That he was ready to move on. That he'd grown up or something," I say.

"It's about being a grown-up?" Paul asks.

"Ask again later," I say. It's my favorite non-answer.

Then I shrug. I wait. I have no idea what "it's" about. But I return week after week in hopes of finding out. One day I'll walk in, and my number will be called, and he'll hand me my fortune, which will tell me everything. I need only to keep showing up. You can't win if you don't play.

I access some of my conversation filler, something along the lines of: Isn't it time to stop screwing around and grow up?

"There's no such thing as 'grown-up,'" Paul says.

"That's encouraging," I say.

"If you really think about it—it *is* encouraging," Paul says.

Silence. I stare at the trees in the park. There is ice on the branches. I can see the skeletons of old bird nests. Every so often the branches catch the wind, like a kite. A visual lullaby. Some ice falls. Then I imagine the cost of pruning those trees. That always breaks the spell. Must be absolutely astronomical.

Peace on Earth and The New Yorker

I LEAVE HIS OFFICE and sit in his waiting room. I'm not quite ready to go home—to mine or my mother's. There is a white noise machine. Four mismatched chairs, one couch, one coffee table. A dysfunctional family of furniture.

On the wall is a small hand-made sign that says: "Please, turn off cell phones in waiting room." I cross out the comma after "Please." It's my way of giving back. This is just one example of my quiet helpfulness.

And suddenly I'm struck with an understanding of why people go to church. It's a lot like this waiting room.

I don't associate it with anything other than dog-eared copies of *The New Yorker*—and quiet waiting. It's a good kind of waiting, because there is no line and the appointment always starts on time. The outside world doesn't knock on the door here. It's genuinely peaceful. Peace on Earth.

My mind travels back to the morning that changed things.

Tin-Foil Swan

I AM IN MY NEW kitchen thinking about myself. I am envying my own life up to this point. I am *that* person. The one who buys the gigantic, shiny coffee-espresso-latte-cappuccino machine in hopes that it will replace or enhance my internal life.

It's not your father's Mr. Coffee . . . no sir! It's the kind of sleek stainless steel "system" that takes up several cubic feet of the pricey Manhattan real estate that is my kitchen counter. Could be worse, I could be a fan of mug caddies. Those spindly little racks that display mugs for people who can't manage the extra effort it takes to put the mugs inside a cabinet. You never want to be too far from your mugs . . . don't want to be separated by prefab cabinetry. Or even a hardwood, such as maple.

When the coffee fad is over—though let's face it, I hope it's not a fad but an accepted addiction that will never be socially demonized—this "system" will not be obsolete.

It's also a hot-water-on-demand machine! Good strategizing, if you ask me. It's too heavy to move, so at least it's also capable of emitting scalding hot water.

I bought it so I'd stay home more. I bought it instead of getting a pet. It's the closest thing to a living being without actually breathing or needing health insurance.

It speaks to me in concise phrases, without prolonged sentences that are weighed down with "ya know" and "at the end of the day" and "basically" and "um" and "like"—which I really appreciate. "Fill water tank. Fill coffee beans." It's direct and to the point. It's one of the most uncomplicated and rewarding relationships I enjoy.

In fact, it was so uncomplicated that I was tempted to complicate it. I wondered, in the wee hours, after my new baby had been unpacked and readied for coffee making in the A.M.—whether the other appliances would be territorial? Jealous? For such a new appliance it certainly was receiving an undeserved amount of space. Of course, the refrigerator wouldn't be able to complain about that! Although the microwave would have a legitimate gripe. Even I recognize that with all of these imaginings, I'm going well out of my way to avoid my internal life. But recognizing it doesn't negate it!

One way I could give my internal life a leg up is by having only one newspaper delivered. But which one would it be? Do I want the *Wall Street Journal* more than I want Page Six of the *Post*? And on the day I have the time to read the whole Sunday *Times,* will that be the first day I don't have home delivery of the Gray Lady? The price of abundance, I'm learning, is constant indecision.

I'm about to enjoy some frothy milk and coffee, read Page Six and at least the front page of the *Times,* when the phone rings.

I look at the coffee machine, in hopes that it might indicate whether or not I should answer the phone. A modern Magic 8-Ball. It doesn't reassure me, so I don't answer. I wait, try to stick to the plan—read my paper, drink my coffee, breathe. *Then* I play the message.

"Tonight," Sam says, "if we're out of there at a reasonable hour, I think we should do . . . something." His voice is sleepy and subdued enough for me to wonder if he's sleep-dialing—acting on some fantasy—and won't remember he's called.

"I've been up since four o'clock waiting for it to be almost six o'clock so I could call you. I just miss you, and I'm really fucking lonely," Sam says. "Lately, when I think about you, and lately it seems like I can't stop—of course it doesn't help that I see you every day—I don't even think about anything great. I keep thinking about that week we were working together in L.A.

"That night I knew you were awake in your room and you wouldn't open the door. And outside of your door I left some steak that the guy at the restaurant wrestled into the shape of a swan. I thought you'd think it was really funny and come looking for me. Every time I think of that I feel like such a jackass. I gave you leftover meat in a fucking tin-foil swan. Why did I think you'd respond to that?"

It's the call I'd been waiting for. What is the worst thing that could have happened if I'd answered the phone? Or opened that door? I would have to *live* my life.

He was right, of course. I was in my hotel room, worrying what hypothetical and amazing thing might happen next, yet afraid to find out. I waited twenty minutes before venturing into the hallway to see what Sam left. The swan. There's only one person in the world who would try to seduce a woman with leftover New York strip—and I let him get away!

Sam has this funny way of seeming more real on the phone than he is in person. Not more real, but more himself. He feels safer the farther away he is. He's like me, in this state of paralyzed limbo. It's the dance of avoidance that happens when your wife leaves you and you meet a woman whose father walked out on her. You are locked in perfect step.

If *it* were going to happen, *it* would have already happened. (Admittedly, even while I'm thinking this, I'm hoping it's not true. It's too simplistic, and when you apply the statement to almost any situation, frankly, it doesn't hold up. I mean, what does its not having happened yet have to do with preventing it from happening in the future? Nothing! Is it a predictor of things to come? Who knows! I don't want the statement to be true, of course. It's just true for now. That gets my hopes up, which just lets me down, so I need to stick with this thinking—you see.)

The Lump

I WANT TO LEAP through the phone and kiss Sam. I want to thank him for being honest about how he feels and the things he regrets. The phone rings again. I skip the small talk. The hellos. I just answer and speak:

"It's not personal. It's situational. I'd be all over you if I didn't have to sit across from you at every meeting," I say. "Let's not forget the Christmas party. One kiss and I get called into HR and am asked to reread and sign the non-fraternization policy again—in front of a witness this time. I felt like I was twelve. My feeling is if I'm working seventy hours a week, and I have the energy to kiss anyone, including a coworker, my stamina should be applauded. I should get some kind of bonus for compartmentalizing my life so beautifully and to the firm's advantage. Our timing has always been off, Sam."

I never go out on a limb, but it feels breezy and wonderful out here; I'm weightless, unburdened! And at the same time it's starting to seem . . . eerily silent.

"Hello?" I say.

I want Sam to reassure me. Tell me that we make our own timing. Everything will be okay.

"Well, kudos to you, honey," my mom says. "That's just good common sense. In my day, relations with a coworker were considered dirty, even cheap."

Of course I don't confess that "dirty" may well be the allure of it. And "cheap" only sweetens the pot.

"Relations?" I say.

"It's none of my business," my mother says. "I wish I'd slept around when I was young and had a different body and done all sorts of things I'd be ashamed of now, too. Who's HR?"

"I'm not sleeping around," I say. I knew no good could come from my answering the phone this early in the morning. Why had I second-guessed myself? Only people on a mission make calls at that hour. The kind of people who have been pacing their kitchen waiting for six-thirty to arrive. There's no adequate preparation for that kind of ambush.

"Emily, you're a grown woman; do as you please," my mom says.

"I am doing as I please. Why are you calling so early? Is something wrong?" I ask.

"You're going to have to call in sick today," Mom says. "I really need you."

The requests for me to call in sick happen regularly and usually mean someone bailed on lunch, or golf, or a spa day. She needs a seat-filler. The notion of paying in full for something she failed to cancel twenty-four hours in advance is one of her bigger beefs.

Someone will pay. Usually, it's me. Even in high school it was an issue. I'd sleep through the alarm and she'd gleefully meet me in the kitchen at ten A.M., asking what "neat" thing we should do that day. I was tardy or absent from nursery school a record forty-seven times . . . and it was only a three-day-a week program. I was a very convenient breakfast companion for my mother.

"I need to go to work today. I could meet you for dinner, or stop by after work," I say. "We're almost finished with this project. I can even take a vacation when it's over. Could we go to Florida?"

"I need someone with me now, right now," Mom says. "I'm dying."

"Dying? Come on, Mom. What is that can't wait until seven o'clock tonight?" I say, getting annoyed.

"Cancer," Mom says. "And I don't want to be alone with it in my living room anymore."

Impersonating Happiness

MY MOTHER HAS never been a reliable narrator of her own story. Once, she had a heart attack. It was the very best kind of heart attack a person can have. It was the kind that happens when a person self-diagnoses—actually misdiagnoses—her own panic attacks. She was immediately given a clean bill of health from a cardiologist. The second, third, and fourth opinions concurred with the first opinion. Out of habit and suspicion, she continued walking around holding her chest for several weeks, while swearing off red meat and chasing down her aspirin with Bordeaux.

My family communicates through extremes: comedy or silence or high drama. Speaking directly, or from the heart, is too "on the money." It would eliminate all the anxiety of a surprise, of nuance. Nuance, it turns out, is very convenient. The perfect scapegoat. You don't necessarily have to mean what you say. You can even pretend to be misunderstood. Humor impersonates happiness.

When my parents told me they were divorcing, they joked about it for weeks. My mother giggled about my father's appearance, his lack of organization, and his inability to dress appropriately without someone's laying out his wardrobe. He wouldn't know how to find his way home, which was fine, since he wasn't welcome to come home anyway.

My father laughed about how my mother would be afraid to leave the apartment without him. All dressed up and too afraid to go. She would have to live her life on the phone, he said. Which was fine since she never stopped talking.

Neither one of them was kidding, and neither one of them was funny. At least not on a topic so close to them or so new to them. Their marriage wasn't—it turns out—a mistake. They were well suited for each other even if they couldn't manage to be happy. They did fit, in that peculiar way that incomplete people sometimes do. They failed in different areas, and when they felt up to it, they picked up the slack and helped each other. Most of the time that worked.

My mother relied on my father's total lack of social awareness to get herself out the door under the guise that she was helping him navigate the world. My father needed structure; he needed to be steered by my mother. He was her confidence, her most practical accessory.

The Davenport

I SAW HER two days ago. She didn't look ill. She looked fantastic. Healthy. She looked like a woman who's had her share of well-researched, age-minimizing treatments, including but not limited to a thoughtful, agonized-over surgical tweak here and there.

As I let myself into her apartment and take my key out of the lock, I call to her: "Mom." I want to hear her voice before I walk in because I fear she may already be dead. I don't want to discover her body in the worst scavenger hunt ever.

She's in the living room, on the davenport, with her legs elevated. She's the only person I know who calls her sofa a davenport. Joanie could never sit on a sofa, or a couch. Joanie relaxes on the davenport. Ice pack on forehead and dressed in new silk pajamas—sea foam green—and a quilted capelet with a fur collar. Matching slippers with heels are placed strategically on the floor next to the davenport so that anyone walking into the room will see that they perfectly complement her well-chosen ensemble. I should be relieved by the visual. So staged and in need of a witness. But I'm not relieved. I've never in my entire life seen my mother in pajamas past seven A.M.

A year and two months after my father left, we started celebrating Christmas again. Very carefully, I woke my mother, eager to rip wrapping paper. She told me to take a shower, brush my teeth and hair, make my bed, and put on a dress first. Then she showered, and watched Mavis the housekeeper make her bed and our breakfast.

It was torture for a six-year-old. I ate at record speed. Loaded the dishwasher. Wiped down the table. Topped off her cup of tea. Then, exhausted from the adrenaline, I'd retreat with her to the living room near lunchtime. At last I was able to open gifts. Neatly. One at a time. As if unwrapping explosives.

Mavis would sit about fifteen feet away from us, watching. She was a witness to our life, including our holidays. Any invitation for her to join us would send her fleeing to her tiny bedroom. When we gave her gifts, she opened them quietly, and in private, the same way she ate her meals.

I see now how foolish it was to think she might be dead. My mother would never die on the davenport. The silk upholstery, with monkeys playing various woodwind instruments, would not set the appropriate dramatic effect that the occasion would call for. She'd die in bed, where her stomach would look flatter. Or in the breakfast room, where the light is especially flattering.

This is what the world looks like when you're raised by people who can't be serious.

"Mom," I say, "I'm here."

"Shhh," Mom says. "I need some sleep, then we'll talk. I've been awake all night."

"You can sleep later," I say. "I need to know what's going on. What kind of cancer? What kind of treatment? When did you find out?"

"Breast cancer," Mom says. "Now let me rest. I've been too terrified to fall asleep. I don't need an interrogation."

"Of course you do! Without an interrogation, I'd get no information at all," I say. "They must have told you more. I'm sure they didn't say you had cancer and then show you to the door."

"Practically," Mom says. "Which was fine with me. It was a brisk sunny day, a nice time for a walk. Better than being told on a rainy day, in my opinion. Besides, what else was there to say—'Here's a pill'? You know I'm not going to be good at this. I have to go to the hospital for tests, classes, monitoring. It's going to take up a lot of time. I don't want to be around sick people. I really don't have time for this right now."

"No one has time for it," I say.

"Oh, you know what I mean. Some people like a project. Like to research and find the newest drug, the best doctors, the latest this, the hottest that. I really just want to enjoy my home, my daughters, take my walks, and have a nice glass of wine at night. I don't need anything else."

"You make it sound like there are people out there volunteering to get cancer," I say. "As if it were a home-renovating project."

"Well, I wasn't trying to offend. I just don't want anything to do with it; that's all," Mom says.

The way she dismisses it makes it sound like dismissing it is an option.

Check here: ( ) Yes, I would like to have cancer.

Or here: ( ) No, thank you. I do not wish to take advantage of the cancer offer at this time.

"On the phone you said you were . . . dying. Did the doctor actually say that?" I ask.

"Well, of course not! That's no way to run a business. People wouldn't pay their bills," Mom says.

That doesn't sound accurate, but she does manage to raise a point that has never occurred to me. It's one of the things I love most about her. Her illumination of how the fringe population thinks.

"So we're not going to talk about it?" I say. "Well, what can I do? How can I help, Mom?"

"Oh, Emily, just be here," Mom says.

"Okay," I say. "I'm here." I hold her hand.

"That's nice, honey," Mom says. "I didn't mean *here,* here. I still need to sleep. Maybe you could go watch TV, or read."

She pulls her silk sleep mask down over her alert eyes.

"Okay," I say. I walk toward her bedroom. I stop and turn. "Mom, I'm really sorry that this is happening to you. I'm sorry if you're scared."

"Okay," she whispers. Her whisper is confident. Why can't I be more like her? Lost in the illusion that life is an illusion? She was awake all night, yet she can't even be bothered to share any details with me now that I am here. Now *I'm* here, all alone in her living room, with her cancer!

I go into her bedroom. I close the door just enough so she won't hear me cry. I sit on a Queen Anne chair and look out the window. I can see the steps of the Met; they are wet from melting snow. We used to have picnics on those steps when I was little.

I'm crying because she's in dire straits and even now we can't have an authentic relationship. And even if I wanted one, I'm fairly certain I'm not capable of having that kind of relationship with her. I feel like I'm hitting a tennis ball against a backboard. The ball keeps bouncing back to me, but I'm the only one working.

Later I poke around her medicine cabinet. There is some Xanax. I check the date on the bottle. Yesterday's date. I shake the bottle. I'm not sure why. There's nothing else of note in her medicine cabinet. No Advil, no Tylenol. Just natural toothpaste and eleven different face creams. All of the pots of cream and tubes of lotion mention that it takes a minimum of thirty days of use for benefits to begin to show . . . like there's a man, woman, or child alive who has the discipline to apply this stuff thirty days in a row.

I try on some of her lipstick and look in the mirror. It does not work on me—too severe. I look at the photographs on her dresser. I don't recognize any of the beautiful people in the photos, and I start to think it's very strange that my mother has so many friends I've never met. All gorgeous. All wearing tuxedos or elegant gowns. Only then do I realize that she never put personal photos in the frames; they still contain the black-and-white stock photos that are displayed in stores. I bought a few of these frames for her. I should have added photos before giving them to her. The distance may be greater than I'd ever thought. There are so many reasons to cry.

Eventually, I go to the kitchen. Open the fridge. I cut up fruit, and while I'm putting it into a bowl, I realize that I have a job and that I never bothered to call my office to say I wouldn't be in today. I never called Sam. I dropped everything and came here.

"It's Emily. Is Sam in?" I ask when his assistant answers.

"Everyone's in the conference room," she says. "They've been in there all morning. Want me to slip him a note?"

"No, thanks, I'll be in," I say. What would the note say exactly? Sorry you poured your heart out on my answering machine and I have not bothered to call back; oh, and my mom has breast cancer: she doesn't speak to her own mother, my sister can't stop shopping long enough to check in, so I'm the only family she has.

I check on my mother, who is now sound asleep. I write a note, telling her that I'll be back soon and that there's fresh fruit in the fridge. I don't want her to wake up while I'm gone and be afraid. I put a framed photo of one of the strangers next to her davenport. To keep watch. It seems like it could be a scene from a horror movie—where the photo comes to life and possibly attacks her. It occurs to me she might wake up startled if the photo is the first thing she sees—so I move it back a respectful distance.

Instant Coffee

THE FACT THAT I forgot I belonged somewhere means something to me. At this moment, it gets me thinking that I really *don't* belong at work.

I walk into the conference room. Gray suits. White shirts. Raised eyebrows and unhappy looks in my direction. I take a seat. I mouth the word "sorry" to everyone who will look. Though some people don't look. They are too incensed that I have the gall to show up late when they've been in this cavernous chamber all morning.

When I first became a lawyer, I loved the extreme detail of it. How language mattered. The way it required my full attention and how, unlike my family, it was explicit in its meaning. I'd found the demanding job that needed me as much as I needed it. It was a dream come true. The family I never had.

With time, you'd think too much of a good thing could only get better. But in my case it's become suffocating. It's devoured all other parts of my life. I couldn't have said this yesterday. I couldn't have admitted it, or maybe it was not yet true yesterday.

I mouth the word "coffee" to Jenny, the assistant. I know what you're thinking—fetch your own coffee, lady. How sexist to expect young and spry Jenny to get coffee. It's the other way around, of course; Jenny gets coffee only for men. In law school, I didn't imagine this would be one of my more difficult precedent-setting arguments. Jenny's paid to be a floater. That means seamlessly filling the gaps. Floating from one task to the next without interrupting the flow of work and ideas. Jenny pretends she doesn't see me. Instead of aiming to be helpful and largely invisible, she pretends I am invisible. I wait until we make eye contact. Then I make a pouring motion. Still, I get the freeze. Jenny looks away from me quickly and begins removing imaginary lint from her skirt. I wait. I pounce again. I mouth the word "coffee," then make a pouring motion, followed by a sipping, oops, too-hot-don't-sip-too-fast motion.

"Jen—," I start to say.

"Jenny! Can you stop pretending you don't see Emily and get the goddamn coffee, so she can quit it with the pantomime routine?" Donald says. "For the life of me I'll never understand how the hell being paid to pour coffee landed on par with abuse."

Donald is a man who does not wait for life, and does not waste time on pleasantries. Donald is a doer. He gets shit done. It must be so satisfying to be Donald.

I can already predict what form the ugly retaliation will take: scalding hot, instant decaf, with nondairy creamer? I miss my coffee machine. I miss my home. I wish it were yesterday instead of today. Too often, that is my wish.

Exit Here

RIGHT AFTER THE MEETING, Sam says: "Rhodes, let's meet in my office."

"Okay, coach," I say.

He doesn't close the door. He leans against his desk.

"I'm sorry," I say.

"What happened?" Sam asks.

I'm imagining what sort of excuse might appease him—or me—in this situation.

I could tell him the truth, but even the truth doesn't quite get me off the hook. I should have called him as soon as my mother fell asleep. I should have called and said, "More tin-foil swans, please."

"You need to talk to me," Sam says. He reaches for my hand and lifts it up to match the palm of my hand against the palm of his hand. Our fingers are stretched out. His hand dwarfs mine. I imagine future generations using this position as a method to determine who might make a suitable mate for life. It's as good a measure as any.

"You know what I was thinking when I was sitting in that meeting?" I say.

"Let me guess. 'Jenny, where the hell's my coffee?'" Sam says.

"Well, that, too. But I was wondering when I decided it was okay for this job to consume my life," I say. "How did work become my central focus? Not my central focus. It's my only focus. I have nothing else."

"That's what happens when you're good at something. You want to spend all of your time doing it," Sam says. "But you've been here for sixty-three days in a row; maybe you just need a break."

He's right. I am good at my job, and being good at something is meaningful. But the more time I spend perfecting what I'm already good at, the less time I spend on things that I'm not good at. You see where this is headed, don't you? A lopsided life. I *do* need a break.

"We both know if I take that *break*—I'm the *girl who needed a break*. It's one more reason for me not to make partner. Partners don't need breaks. I'm living under the constant threat of not making partner. It used to seem kind of exciting and elusive. Like hunting. Now it just makes me feel bad," I say. "I'm thirty years old. My mother just told me she has cancer. Why am I spending all of my time here?"

"Cancer? Oh, Emily. I'm sorry," Sam says. "How is she coping?"

"It's hard to describe," I say. I've never been able to describe her accurately and now is no different.

"I really am sorry. Please let me know if there's any way I can help," Sam says.

"Thanks," I say.

"About you and me, Em," Sam says. "This morning, I pretty much laid it all out there—on the phone. The woman who has never been tardy or sick in four years chooses today as the day not to show up. Doesn't even call. If you were me, what would you make of that?" Sam asks.

"Everything is different today," I say. I want to claim some newfound ability to see things more clearly. But it's not true. I just see things differently.

He drops my hand. Not sure why he held it, just to let it go. A subliminal reinforcement of what I'm doing to him? Mano a mano. Very cagey, amigo. His directness is startling and frightening and exciting. It's also completely foreign to me.

I stare at him.

"The thing that's always concerned me about you is that you live your life with one foot out the door. It's unsettling," Sam says. "Worse than that, it's familiar. It reminds me of Susanna."

Okay, that is officially the most hurtful thing he's ever said to me. I think I might cry because it also happens to be true. I do live with one foot out the door. But if I cry, he wins, right? I'm not sure what he wins exactly. The satisfaction of articulating my dysfunction better than I can? All I know is I can't lose this one. Maybe I really am a lawyer at heart. Why is winning even part of this exchange?

"That's really unnecessary and really unfair," I say. "I've made solid decisions in my life so I don't *have* an ex-spouse to compare *you* to."

"You're right. No ex-spouse for you," Sam says, smiling.

"Why are you smiling?" I say.

"A spouse, or even an ex-spouse, would have required you to have made a commitment to someone," Sam says. "That's not an area of strength for you, is it?"

He takes a deep breath and walks away from me, toward the window.

"I'm sorry. I really am. I didn't mean for this conversation to head in this direction. Emily, I've thought for a long time that we were going to end up together, so I didn't really care so much about the when of it. Now, though, the long road is starting to seem like the infinite road."

"You don't get to pin this on me," I say. "It's really convenient. But do you know how many times we've canceled
plans because of this place?" I say. "You're no more ready
to have a relationship than I am."

"You're completely wrong about that," Sam says. "We're
almost finished with this project. Let's go skiing. Maybe
Vermont or Lake Placid?"

Negotiating 101. He's calling my bluff.

"So we can live our life on vacation a few weeks each
year?" I say.

The more I stand there, the more resentful I become. I
hate it that I never leave my office when it's light out. I hate
it that I spend my weekends stressing about what will be
sitting on my desk come Monday. I hate that the lines have
become so blurry that I don't know if I'm a workaholic, or if
I'm using this job as an excuse to spend time with Sam or
as an excuse to avoid spending time with Sam away from
work.

"You're quitting your job, aren't you?" Sam asks.

"Yes," I say.

"Grow up!" Sam says, slamming the door. For privacy?
Too late for that. Anyone not watching us before is watching now that the door has been slammed. "That's not how
you quit a job!"

"It's my job, I'll quit how ever I want to quit," I say. If
I'd thrown in a "nah-nah-nah," the regression would be
complete.

He stares at me for a few seconds. It seems like days. I feel like collapsing and crying. Just getting it all out.

"Emily, you're supposed to quit the shitty things in your life, not the good things," Sam says, walking toward me.

He's right about that. All those years in school and no one ever mentioned practical life and how to manage it. The topic never even came up. That's beyond an oversight. It's blasphemous. What do I need to know about statistics and Latin when I don't even know the basics about how to interact with other people?

I know what I'm doing, and I still can't stop. I've studied my mother's communication style my whole life. I feel stuck with it. I could see the disbelief on Sam's face when I was talking to him. He was incredulous and angry. I never learned how to be either one. His responses are appropriate. It's foreign and terrifying and endearing.

His arms are around me. I stand still, absorbing the closeness for a few seconds so I can refer to it later when I start regretting my next move. I step away from him, open the door, and race down the hall. Tears well up in my eyes, and I wait until I'm in the elevator before I start crying.

I push the button for the lobby, and then start sobbing. A tissue is being waved over my shoulder. So much for being alone.

"Thanks, Donald," I say.

Falling in Love

LOST PEOPLE ARE DIFFERENT. They will drive around in the same circle over and over rather than try a new path. Their fear of getting more lost paralyzes them into staying lost in the area that's just become familiar. It supersedes their ability to chart a new course. They circle and backtrack and stay comfortably lost because it's less scary than seeing something different than what's presently in front of them.

The weekend I fell for Sam happened over a year ago. He was still married. We were all working at the same firm—me, Sam, and Susanna. They invited me to their house in East Hampton for the weekend. Sam had a broken ankle. Men over thirty-five have a way of kidding themselves and thinking it's a good idea to play pick-up basketball with men under the age of thirty-five.

Susanna and I walked from Lee Street, over to Lily Pond Lane, and down to Main Beach. We left Sam and his ankle behind. It was cold and sunny. The air seemed so clean. It's the kind of day that seems like nothing can go wrong.

"We're getting divorced," Susanna said.

"Good one," I said.

"No, really. We are," Susanna said.

"You seem like you're . . . together," I said.

"Oh, I haven't told him yet!" Susanna said.

"Then why are you telling *me*?" I asked.

"I had to tell someone," Susanna said.

"*Someone?*" I said.

"I'm dreading it. He's a really good guy," she said.

"Work things out," I said.

It's shocking, in hindsight, that I felt so free to give advice I could never implement myself.

"It's too late. I'm moving to Chicago," Susanna said.

"Who's in Chicago?" I asked.

She didn't answer. Maybe no one was in Chicago. Maybe Chicago was her clean slate. What am I saying? Brutal winters. Chicago can *only* mean someone else.

I was staying in their first-floor guest room. I woke up in the middle of the night. I could hear a car starting. Then a loud thud and some swearing. I walked into the living room.

"Ouch! Son of a bitch!" Sam said; as he bent to lift some firewood that he dropped, he tripped over the track of the sliding-glass door. More firewood fell, and a log landed on his bad ankle, knocking him to the floor.

It was painful to watch. So I turned away.

"Hey, are you going to be okay?" I said, still not looking.

"Yeah, yeah, I'm okay," Sam said. "You can look. Did I wake you? Of course I woke you. Sorry. I thought maybe you'd left with Susanna."

"Susanna left?" I asked, turning toward Sam.

"Yes," Sam said, "she left."

We crawled around on the floor together, picking up

firewood. When we were finished, still on our hands and knees, his face was close to mine. In that moment, he seemed like he'd be an easy person to be married to. But what do I know?

"Thanks," he said.

"Sure," I said.

"I mean thanks for not asking questions about why one of your hosts left at midnight," Sam said.

I keep expecting to hear her car in the driveway. She won't be on the road five minutes before she realizes what a mistake she's made, and who she has given up.

I went back to the guest room and stared at the ceiling and eventually fell asleep.

At two A.M. I heard some cabinets opening and closing in the kitchen. I brushed my teeth and went out to take a look.

"Can I help with something?" I asked.

"I'm making waffles. Want some?" Sam said.

"Sure," I said.

"Did you know she was moving to Chicago?" Sam said.

"I really like waffles," I said. "Where do you get a heart-shaped waffle iron?"

"Wedding gift," Sam said.

I look at the floor. "Oh," I said. "She's making a mistake."

"Maybe. Maybe not," Sam said. "But thanks."

"My grandmother used to have a maple tree in her backyard," I said. "About two feet from the ground there was a spout sticking out of the tree, and we'd leave a cup under the spout overnight and collect the maple sap the next day. I remember reading that one tree can produce forty to eighty gallons of sap a year."

Are you starting to understand why I work sixty hours a week and don't have an active romantic life?

"I'm sorry. I know what you're thinking."

"What was I thinking?" Sam says.

"For the love of God, lady, let me eat my waffles in peace," I said.

"No. I was thinking I was glad I invited my aunt to the wedding," Sam said. "I think she gave us the waffle maker."

I washed the dishes. Sam dried them. It was three-thirty in the morning, and that was the most fun I'd had in a long time.

"I should get to bed," Sam said. "Rest this ankle."

"Oh. Okay," I said. I didn't want him to go to bed. I wanted to stay up all night and talk. I can remember the sound of my own disappointment— Oh, okay. I was embarrassed by it. I was having a lot of fun while his marriage was falling apart.

"Hey, we can keep talking. I have to get my foot elevated, though. I can lie here on the couch. I probably wouldn't be able to fall asleep anyway," Sam said.

There are five bedrooms in the house. He fell asleep on the couch with his ankle raised. I fell asleep on a chair with a robe draped over me.

Onboard Navigation

ON SUNDAY AFTERNOON I drive us back to the city in his car. I turn onto Route 27 and think about things I am grateful for . . . at the top of the list is a broken ankle and women who make bad decisions. Why did my good luck have to come from someone else's bad luck? There must be a finite supply of luck, I decide.

Sam starts to punch our destination into the onboard navigation system. Happiness? Contentment? New York City, actually. The navigation system speaks. It has a British accent. I distrust it immediately. It sounds too smooth. Like a player.

"I know where I'm going," I say. "I don't need that."

"If there's traffic, we might need an alternate route," Sam says.

"I'm surprised you'd trust a computer to get you from point A to point B," I say.

"Ah, the lady has trust issues," Sam says.

"Not really," I say. Trust issues doesn't do my extreme phobia justice.

"A computer has no motivation to send me down the wrong path," Sam says.

I've made a rather large error here, I realize. Without meaning to I've revealed one of my more unattractive traits.

"Why are my hands hot?" I say.

"I think the steering wheel heater is on," Sam says. He pushes a button that turns off the heat on the steering wheel.

"Does that mean that the rest of the car was so perfect that they had time to tinker with the small stuff? Or did they spend way too much time on novelty items and now I have to worry that a tire might pop off?" I say.

"You watched a lot of cartoons as a kid, didn't you? Tires don't pop off," Sam says.

We hit traffic on 27, and I request an alternate route. The British voice starts spewing commands. My peripheral vision tells me Sam is engrossed in a contract markup. The navigational voice precedes nearly everything he says with an "if possible." If possible, make a U-turn ahead. If possible, take the next left. If possible? Where was this voice when I needed it? Where was this voice when I was making all those wrong turns in my twenties?

"Take the next turn on your left in two hundred yards." I ignore the command. It makes no sense. That can't possibly be correct. But the voice is unbending. "If possible, make a U-turn ahead." I ignore it again. Hoping it'll go away or assume I made the turn already. But no, this Brit is determined. "If possible, make a U-turn ahead. If possible, make a U-turn ahead. If possible, make a U-turn ahead."

We are in dirt-road territory at this point. We're venturing into the uncharted areas of Long Island. We are literally off the map. The voice gave up a few minutes ago. The navigation screen reads "Return to public road. Do not proceed. Make U-turn."

"Okay!" I say.

"Are you looking for a place to turn around?" Sam asks, looking up from his papers.

"No," I say. "I think I can squeeze between those trees."

"If I'd known we were going off-roading, I'd have worn a cup," Sam says.

I stop the car. I back up about sixty feet and turn the car around.

The voice returns. "Left turn ahead," it says.

"Is it me, or does the voice sound a little suspicious?" I ask. "Almost sounds like he's winging it and making stuff up as we go along."

"You're the one who landed us in the middle of the woods—not him," Sam says.

"So you were listening to that whole conversation we were having?" I say.

"Yes," Sam says.

I make a left turn. I follow the verbal commands of the navigation system. We're out of the woods in no time and back on 27. No more adventures in mistrust for me. Two hours later we're in Manhattan.

"You have arrived at your destination," the voice says.

Carlyle Hotel

SAM IS STAYING at the Carlyle for two nights. Susanna says her clothing will be packed and she'll be in Chicago by Tuesday. Quick. Simple. Or quick, anyway.

"Thanks for driving. It was an interesting route. I've never been in the middle of the Pine Barrens," Sam said.

"What can I say, I'm fun to have around," I said.

"Yeah, you are. Want to have a quick dinner?" Sam asked.

"Sure," I said.

We're in the bar. We order red wine and burgers and water. Between the time we sit down and the time we order, something changed.

"You just realized you're getting divorced, didn't you?" I asked.

"Yeah," Sam said. "I was thinking that this is a lot of fun. I should come here more often. Then I remembered that I'm staying here for a few nights because my wife is moving out. Wow."

"I'm sorry. I really am," I said.

"Thanks," Sam said.

"Should I change the subject? Or should I try to trash-talk Susanna?" I asked.

"Change the subject," Sam said.

"Okay. Single greatest movie ever made?" I asked.

"No contest," Sam said.

"*Lawrence of Arabia*?" I said. "Wait. You're a guy. You'll say it's *The Godfather*."

"You're sexist, and you're not even close! *Everyone* knows *Citizen Kane* is the finest film ever made," Sam said.

"Completely forgot about that one," I said.

" 'A fellow can remember a lot of things you wouldn't think he'd remember. You take me. One day back in 1896, I was crossing over to Jersey on the ferry. And as we pulled out, there was another ferry pulling in. And on it there was a girl waiting to get off. A white dress she had on,' he says. 'I saw her for only one second. She didn't see me at all. But I'll bet a month hasn't gone by since that I haven't thought of that girl,' " Sam said.

"How on earth do you remember that?" I said.

"How do you ever forget it?" Sam said.

It's what happens when loss is always there with you. When you see the antidote to the loss, the moment becomes palpable and illuminated. You can't avoid knowing it is in the room with you. The idea that a life's wound could be healed is exciting treachery. Too good to be true.

I'm Not a Waitress

I'VE ACCOMPLISHED A LOT for one day. I trashed my career *and* left an amazing man in the lurch. If I put my mind to it, maybe I can cure Mom's cancer today, too. Tomorrow I'll pace myself.

Mom is still seated on the davenport with a photograph of an anonymous male model watching over her. It looks as though she has not moved since I left the apartment. But she must have. She's wearing another new outfit. Reading glasses rest on her nose. In her left hand is a glass of champagne; in her right hand is the phone. On her lap are several opened address books, including one dating back to the seventies.

"Maryanne, it's Joanie. I hope you're well. I have cancer. Give me a ring when you have a few minutes; I could use some cheering up. They say they caught it early, but I'm sure they say that to everyone," my mom says. She hangs up. She starts dialing another number using the eraser end of a pencil so she doesn't maul her recent manicure.

"Who's Maryanne?" I ask.

"She used to do my highlights until her arthritis got too bad. Now she's babysitting her grandchildren. For money," Mom says.

"Beats touching people's hair all day," I say.

On the upside, when my mom needs something, she doesn't hesitate to ask. On the downside, it's rare that she doesn't need something. She'll call friends to tell them she's lost her keys and ask if they have any ideas where she should look for them. In her game book, there's no such thing as *too* passive-aggressive.

Mom gives me the international shut-up-I'm-on-the-phone sign. She holds the phone to her ear and covers her other ear with a pillow as if to drown out a shuttle launch.

"Richard! Joanie here. Bad news. I have cancer," Mom says. She nods a few times. Her face starts to smile.

"How sweet of you! Yes, I'd love company," Mom says. "What stage? I have no idea. Hold on, I have all the details written down somewhere. Honey, grab my papers for me." I hand her a notebook. She glances at the pages and speaks into the phone again. "Stage one. Okay, I'll see you soon." She hangs up the phone.

"How many people have you called?" I ask.

"I really couldn't guess. I've been at it a while. Would you like some champagne?" Mom says.

"Sure," I say. I walk to the kitchen to get a champagne glass.

"While you're in there, can you get the ladder and the mop?" Mom asks.

"Yes," I say. I find the ladder, the mop, and a glass and return to the living room.

"Stage one?" I say. "In this situation that's good news, right? Great news, even?"

"Yes, great news!" my mom says with zeal and annoyance. "Do you see that smudge up there? It's been driving me crazy since yesterday. Life is too short to have to look at dirty windows!"

"Life is too short to waste time cleaning windows or even to be thinking about windows," I say.

My mother climbs up the ladder to the fifth rung. She's

wearing jeans, a blue cashmere sweater, and matching driving moccasins. Her hair is up. She's wearing lapis teardrop earrings and a lapis beaded necklace. Her nails are freshly painted with a shade of red called I'm-Not-A-Waitress. She's tipsy and climbing ladders.

I'm sitting on her couch, reading a magazine.

"Are you sure I can't do that for you?" I ask.

"I'm enjoying this," Mom says. "It's therapeutic."

"As much as I hate to steal your joy, it really doesn't seem safe," I say.

"Did I get them clean?" Mom asks. "Can you see any streaks from there? I can't stand the idea of strangers looking around the apartment and seeing dirt. I wouldn't want anyone to think I didn't care."

"What strangers are hypothetically judging you now?" I ask, not looking up.

"When I'm gone, you and your sister aren't going to want to keep this place. Are you? Maybe you do want this place. Well, if you girls decide to keep it, consider the clean windows to be an extra gift," Mom says.

"You aren't going to die. Strangers aren't going to be walking through your home. It sounds like they caught it very early. You should be thinking about renovating this place, not about selling it," I say. "No one has avocado-colored appliances anymore. It's like a KitchenAid museum in here. Seriously, who knew those appliances would last so long?"

"Longer than me, you mean?" Mom says.

"Your mantra should be Stage One Cancer Is Curable. You're more likely to die from making bad decisions like getting buzzed and climbing a ladder to clean windows," I say.

"So according to your mantra, I still die—just not of cancer?" Mom says.

The doorman buzzes. Mom dismounts the ladder and answers the intercom.

"Yes, send him up," Mom says.

My mother disappears from the room. She comes back wearing more lipstick, and climbs back up the ladder. Very casually, she turns toward me.

"Do I have lipstick on my teeth?" Mom asks.

"No," I say.

"Emily, I just want you to know that I've been in such a state. The oncologist told me not to make any important decisions for a few days. That's easy for him to say. He's not dying! I may have only a little while . . . am I supposed to sit on my hands and do nothing?" Mom says. "I'll say one thing about cancer. It's really grounded me."

There's a knock at the door.

"Who's here?" I ask.

"Can you be a good helper and grab the door?" Mom replies.

"I haven't been a good helper since I was five," I say.

I open the door. Initially, I am confused. I think he might have accidentally knocked on the wrong door. What are the chances of that happening, though?

The awkward stranger standing at the door is my father, Jim. I haven't seen Joanie and Jim in the same room since my high school graduation. They refused to make eye contact or speak or appear together in any photographs.

For a while after they split I saw him every other year, on Christmas Eve. We broke that awkward tradition when I left for college.

"Hi. What's going on?" I ask.

We shake hands. We're clumsy strangers.

"Your mother called me, said that she was very ill and that she needed to see me," Jim says. "Where is she? Is she still . . ."

"Alive? Yes, very much so. Come on in," I say.

My mother continues cleaning windows as if she hasn't called her ex-husband, as if the doorman hadn't told her my father was there to see her, as if she hadn't just put on fresh lipstick!

"Joanie," he says, sounding bereft when he notices her standing on the ladder. "What the hell are you doing? Shouldn't you be hospitalized?"

Yes! She should be hospitalized.

"Hello!" Mom says. "How nice of you to come. It's so important to be surrounded by those you loved at a time like this. I forgive you, and I want you to know that. That's really all I have to say."

The words are supposed to sound cool and casual. Instead, she sounds like she's reading from a script that

she's just seeing for the first time. "Important to be surrounded by those you *loved* at a time like this?"

At no point does she make a move to step down from
the ladder. She keeps cleaning and doesn't bother to look
in his direction.

"I'm so sorry to hear your news," Jim says. "If there's
any way I can help, please let me know."

"Well, there is this one spot, about six inches out of my
reach," Mom says, finally looking at him.

He makes a move toward the ladder, smiling.

"Wait, where's the camera?" I say.

"In the kitchen," Mom says. "Near the silverware."

"It was a joke," I say.

"It's almost reassuring how nothing has changed," Jim
says.

He doesn't know either one of us well enough to know
if nothing's changed.

She hands him the mop and proceeds to boss him
around for twenty minutes or so. Then the doorbell rings
again. Mr. Simone. Our neighbor from twenty years ago is
here to say his good-byes. Mom apparently went through
the Rolodex and is parading her past before her eyes. It explains the fresh manicure. The hair foils in the bathroom
trash can. The shopping list on the counter: *Guest book. Linen
napkins. Cotton gloves? Cigars for the men. New highball glasses.*

It's all so apropos for a girl who has chosen to live in
the past.

Good-bye. Hello.

I WALK MY FATHER downstairs. We shake hands again. I don't know a single other person on the planet who has this kind of warped relationship with a blood relative. Except my sister Marjorie.

"Well, I guess, maybe I'll see you around," I say.

"Okay, I'll see you, then," Jim says. Then he leans forward and kisses my head.

"Okay," I say.

We're both being polite. But I'm not sure why. If I spoke the truth, what's the worst thing that could happen to me? He wouldn't speak to me? We're already not speaking.

"Perhaps we could have lunch sometime," Jim says. "You could come to the office."

"Sure. Sometime," I say.

"How about Friday?" Jim says. "Come on Friday, around one o'clock."

"Okay," I say. "Friday. If Mom doesn't have any doctor appointments."

I return to my mother's apartment. She's drinking tea and leafing through an address book from the go-go eighties. Mr. Simone is in the kitchen making her dinner.

"Why didn't you tell me you called Jim?" I ask.

"I'm a woman of mystery. I don't tell you everything," Mom says.

And yet she rarely stops speaking. She talks, and talks, as a diversion. The fact is that she reveals almost nothing. How does she manage not to reveal more purely by accident?

"When did I stop calling Jim 'Dad'?" I ask.

"It was early on," Mom says. "Four, maybe five years old."

"Why do you suppose that is?" I ask.

"I just assumed you saw him for what he was," Mom says.

"And what is he?" I ask.

"A nice enough man who never really understood how to be a father," Mom says. "Or a husband. Or, well, he wasn't much of a cook either. He thought he was. They all do. I could go on and on. Of course, he also has a very charming side."

Red Wet-Look Boots

WHEN I WAS FOUR or five, my father would slap Aqua Velva onto my cheeks after he shaved. He smacked it on so hard it stung my skin, but I still waited for it most mornings. Waited for that connection.

The only other memory I have from that time is very vivid. I am five, and I am standing out in front of our church after Sunday school. Everyone else has gone home;

I am the last one waiting. It was not unusual for me to be the afterthought.

My father arrives. I wave. He tells me to sit in the car. He has to run inside for something. His soul? It was suspicious.

A long time passes; it's hot, and I'm tired of waiting in the car. So I go inside. It's quiet. There's no one in the rectory. I walk around, opening doors, searching. I smell church smells. I see a communion wafer on the counter, in the kitchen. Its surface feels like velvet. There is a cross in the center of it. I slip it into my pocket.

I walk by the empty Sunday-school classrooms. And then I get to my classroom, and I see him. My father. He's kissing Miss Murray, my Sunday-school teacher. So that's what he forgot! To kiss my teacher! He's pressed against her, near the sink where we wash out the paintbrushes. She has her arms around him. And he's unbuttoned the front of her shirt halfway. She's wearing red wet-look boots, yet manages to look wholesome. I covet those boots.

I knock at the door and run—black patent leather Mary Janes hitting linoleum—for the car, where I pretend to be asleep.

None of My Business

I'm in my mother's bathtub eating a grape Popsicle that tastes kind of like frozen lamb chops. There was no expiration date on the wrapper. Frozen water with imitation flavoring and colors never go bad, but they do start to absorb their surroundings—just like the rest of us.

Mom walks in. A careful, hopeful smile on her face. True joy in her eyes. Is it the doctor? Is he calling to say it's all a big mistake? He was reading someone else's films?

"Paul something or other," Mom says, holding out the phone. Then covering the receiver, "Is he the one from the office?"

"I'm taking a bath," I say.

"I see that. I could take a message, but he says he's returning your call," Mom says, smiling some more.

I transfer the Popsicle to the other hand and take the phone.

"Should I close the door?" Mom asks.

"Please," I say.

She closes the door reluctantly and not all the way. She's visibly excited at the prospect that this might be "the one from the office." I'm sure she'd be much less excited to know that I called my shrink for an emergency session. So panicked was I by the prospect of another parent leaving me that I called him and left a rather hysterical message.

"Hi," I say. "Thanks for calling back."

"Finally got to speak to the famous Joanie," Paul says.

"Very exciting stuff," I say.

"Do you want to talk now, or would you like to come in tomorrow?" Paul says.

"Tomorrow," I say. Hearing his voice is a relief. The Popsicle is running down my hand. "Because I'm pretty sure my mom is listening at the door."

"Okay," Paul says. "I have an opening at ten."

"Great. Thanks," I say. I hang up the phone.

I hear movement on the other side of the door.

"I just wondered if you needed a towel," Mom says.

"There's one on the towel bar," I say. "If you have a question, just ask."

"Okay. Who's Paul?" Mom asks. Smiling some more.

"My shrink," I say.

"Oh. Well, that's none of my business," Mom says. "Is he any good? A lot of them have no idea what they're doing."

Dreaming

I HAVE A DREAM about Sam. I'm at his apartment making dinner. But I can't find anything that I need to prepare the meal. So he has to find everything. He finds the salt, the good knives, the spatula, the place mats—everything. All I do is cook. I feel lost in his house, but I don't want to leave.

Paul

I DON'T SIT DOWN in the black pleather club chair; I fall down. I'm going to have to say this aloud, aren't I? It will be real and true. And then I start crying. Sobbing actually. I've never done this here. It takes me a while to get the courage to look at him.

"My mother is dying," I say. "She has breast cancer." I start crying at this part again, and the room's all blurry from my tears.

"Goodness. What have the doctors said about it?" Paul asks. "Is that what she said? She said she's dying?"

"Yes," I say.

"In those words?" Paul asks.

"Yes," I say. It's quintessential Mom.

"I hope that's not the case. But I think you should speak with her doctor, don't you? I think you should speak with her doctor and find out what her diagnosis is, and what her treatment will be like," Paul says. "You can't be in control of her health, but knowing what comes next would be helpful. Cancer generally happens in stages. If it's caught early, she's very likely to live a long life."

"You're right. I'll call her doctor. This only happened yesterday," I say. "My sister is not helpful at all. She's pregnant and can't be bothered to get involved. She says my mother is strong and she'll get through it."

"Okay, so your sister is either in denial or dislikes your

mother. We can focus only on you. How have *you* been coping?" Paul asks.

"Not well," I say.

"Not well, how?" Paul says.

"I quit my job, walked out on Sam, and slept at my mom's house last night," I say.

Long pause. I'm actually waiting for him to shake his head in disgust, or laugh hysterically. He does neither.

"All or nothing," Paul says. "All or nothing. Finding that middle ground would . . ."

"Be impossible, but feel like a vacation?" I say.

"It would be very valuable," Paul says. "You have an immediate situation that needs attention, and I really think you'd benefit from coming here more often. Less hiding."

"Exactly!" I say.

Hiding is what I'm all about. He wants to strip that away. I hate it that I can't have a crisis that isn't accompanied by a sales pitch for more sessions. But I'm simultaneously flattered that my situation is so dire that he wants to see me more often.

But I loathe the idea that he'll soon see through my treading-water tactics with him. It's taken two years to learn to trust Paul, alone in this room. Now he wants me to show up more often? Make a bigger commitment?

"Thanks for the invite. It's always nice to be asked," I say.

"Why not try one extra session?" Paul says. "It's not like you can hide behind work anymore."

When I don't say anything, he adds: "With issues come solutions. You'd welcome them more if you saw it that way."

"Oh, please, no one ever resolves anything," I say.

"If you believed that you wouldn't be here," Paul says.

The Crazy Filter

AT MY MOTHER'S INSISTENCE, I sleep in my childhood room. There's no nostalgia here. It looks nothing like the room I had as a child because within twelve hours of my leaving for college, Mom gave the thumbs-up to the wrecking ball and had the room redecorated. The theme of the room is now "Island." The bed is made of bamboo. The wallpaper is green with a paler shade of green creating a grid. There are pastel-colored silhouettes of palm trees. The rug is sand-colored. Above the bamboo dresser is a mirror decorated with seashells. Evidence of the first eighteen years of my life fit neatly into two brown boxes in the closet.

I lie here trying to fall asleep and miss my own apartment. I didn't go through co-op board approval and get myself into serious debt to sleep *here*. I miss my very soft, plain white sheets, my own pajamas, and the possibility of being home to answer the phone in the unlikely event that Sam calls.

I finally fall asleep around three A.M. It's still dark outside when I hear a frightening sound. The curtains and blackout shades are squeakily opened. I feel like I've been blindfolded and held in solitary confinement. My eyes actually hurt from the light and lack of sleep.

"What time is it?" I ask.

"Five-thirty," Mom says. "It's just so good to have you here. Back in your own room. I can't wait!" Mom says. She's moved down to the carpeting. She's in spandex, seated in a child's pose. She has a pencil in hand, and has folded the *Times* so she can work on a crossword puzzle while we pretend to talk.

"Can't wait for what?" I ask.

There is a tray by her feet, on it is a glass of orange juice and a fleshy mosaic of too many vitamins. Her eyes dart around the crossword puzzle.

"Here are your vitamins and some juice," Mom says. "No pulp, the way you like it!"

I like pulp but don't mention this. I'm not sure why. I don't want to disappoint her. Don't want her to think less of herself for not knowing that I enjoy pulp. Part juice. Part fruit. Win. Win.

"I take one multivitamin with extra calcium. I don't take a dozen vitamins," I say.

"Can't have too many antioxidants," Mom says. It sounds like a threat.

I stare at the tray. I can't possibly choke down all of those pills. I'd just feel bad for my liver, expecting it to process all of them at once. If I'm going to ask great things of my organs, I like to butter them up for a few days with greens and lots of water. I save the overtime requests for the very memorable—such as great wine. Not a fistful of fortified chalk and oil.

"I'll take them after I eat," I say.

"We're doing a juice fast today," Mom says.

"After we eat?" I ask.

She's opening dresser drawers and unfolding pressed pillowcases. Then she refolds them—perfectly. She does it again. I worry this might be what she does all day when I'm not around.

Last week, she was practicing her deathbed scene on the davenport. This week she is an overzealous juicer who wants to reorganize her drawers. Her mood is remarkably upbeat compared to the day I got here, when she felt pretty strongly that she didn't have the time or the interest to fight cancer or learn the nuances of her own diagnosis. Now she is a superhero. Ready for anything. Armed with juice and a good attitude. Somewhere, in there, is my mom.

She moves on from the folding of pillowcases, and starts making the bed while I'm still in it. She fluffs the pillow and straightens the bed skirt. She hasn't made my bed since I was five. Even then, Maris did it, but Mom fluffed the pillows. You know, that final touch.

"Can you get up so I can make the bed?" Mom says. "It's hard to work around you. I like to have all the beds made before I go out."

"I know," I say. "I remember when you'd wake me up so my bed could be made so that you could leave the house."

"I never did that," Mom says, smiling.

"You just did it now," I say.

"I could help you pack today," Mom says. "We could go to the box store after our walk. They have everything you could want, at least as far as boxes go."

"Pack for what?" I say. Besides, boxes should be free.

"For when you move back in," Mom says. Her face changes here. She's terribly disappointed that I don't know what she's talking about. She's hurt. I never said I'd move back in with her. Yes, I've been sleeping here, but move back in?

"I'm not moving back in," I say. "I thought I'd stay with you for a few nights and help out. I live only nine blocks away. I can be here when you need me. I've quit my job. I'm available whenever you call now."

I should have had the foresight to buy twenty blocks away, like Marjorie.

"Oh," Mom says, starting to leave the room. The fantasy about the trip to the box store is all behind her now.

"Wait a minute. Stop. When did I say I was moving back in?" I ask.

"Last week," Mom says.

"I never said that," I say.

"You asked what I needed. I said I needed you here. You said okay. I didn't expect you to give up your life and move back home, but you offered, and I accepted," Mom says. "You've been here night and day. Why would you be spending the night if you weren't planning to live here?"

"That is just so interesting," I say.

I feel like I'm talking, and over my words she lays the big old crazy filter, and suddenly she hears something different from what I said. It's been happening for three decades.

"It'll be just like old times," Mom says. "You can help me clean out my closets; that way you won't have to do it alone."

"I think we need to work on being more optimistic. I know you're scared, but your own doctor said the patients he'd seen in your situation all live very long lives," I say.

"I love Dr. Kealy, you know I do. But he can't be more than forty years old. Who knows what his definition of long life is? Fifty? Sixty, tops," Mom says.

She's serious. She wants me to move back home.

"I remember how you used to like to throw cold water on me when I was in the shower . . ." I say.

"Only when you were overdoing it," Mom says. "Long showers are a mistake."

"Why?" I ask.

She doesn't elaborate.

"Why?" I ask again.

"I'm going to make a smoothie," Mom says.

"I like pulp, by the way," I say.

"No, you don't, and you never have," Mom says. "So if you like it now, you're just being disagreeable."

She's good! For a split second there, I thought maybe I didn't like pulp.

Life Coach versus Food Coach

WE'RE AT MARJORIE'S table at Le Bilboquet. My sister is eighteen months older than I am. I was the tomboy, and Marjorie could keep a bow in her hair all day. She didn't own sneakers. Cried when my mother tried to buy them for her. A detail that always troubled me.

"How did you become a socialite exactly?" I ask.

"I don't know, but the pressure is getting to me," Marjorie says. "I'm still going out five nights a week. It's crazy. I can't even fit at this table anymore. This is so depressing."

"You're pregnant. Cut yourself some slack. Start staying home at night," I say.

"There's just too much going on to stay home and, on top of all that, Dory and Nevin disagree constantly," Marjorie says.

"Few things are as troubling as when your life coach and your food coach are feuding," I say. "Seriously, who among us could choose sides?"

"And I'm stuck in the middle," Marjorie says.

"A person with two watches never knows what time it is," I say. "Fire one of them."

"Easy for you to say," Marjorie replies.

"You're right. Fire both of them," I say. "This is why you have no money, by the way. Which I know was going to be your next question. They keep signing you up for things you can't afford, and you keep saying yes."

"You really care about me, don't you?" Marjorie says. "No one else talks to me like that."

"*I* don't talk to anyone else like that," I say. It's a relief to speak the blunt truth, and to be loved for it instead of loathed.

"I'm so emotional right now, and I hate Malcolm," Marjorie says. "You know what I caught him doing this morning?"

"What?" I ask.

"Sitting down to pee!" Marjorie says.

"That son of a bitch!" I say.

"It's not funny," Marjorie says.

"Well . . ." I say.

"I'm about to have a baby. I need someone strong. Not a man who sits to pee," Marjorie says, looking like she may cry.

"Maybe his willingness to sit to pee means he's the ultimate male. Not afraid of stereotypes and posturing," I say. "Why should men have to stand up to pee?"

"He called you, didn't he? He told you to say that!" Marjorie says.

"I've been at Sloan-Kettering all morning with Mom," I say. "She had some pre-op testing, and she's really into the relaxation workshops. I think she has a crush on someone in the class. The lumpectomy happens in a few weeks."

"I'm really sorry. I've been talking about myself the

whole time," Marjorie says. "How is Mom doing? She hasn't told me anything. Keeps saying she doesn't want me to stress out while I'm pregnant. How big is the tumor?"

"Size of a pea," I say.

"I was going to ask which food they compared it to—orange, grapefruit, cantaloupe. Worried it would sound insensitive," Marjorie says.

"You? Insensitive?" I say.

"A pea is good news," Marjorie says, brightening.

"That's what her oncologist said, too," I say. "But it's still hard to get excited about good-bad news. I need to work on that, I guess."

"How's she handling it?" Marjorie asks.

"She's in intense organizing mode," I say. "Meaning very worried."

"What about you?" Marjorie says.

"Melancholy half of the time," I say. "Annoyed the other half. But most of the time, you know, things are remarkably the same, which is both comforting and kind of a shame."

"It sounds like things are going well, all things considered," Marjorie says. "Especially if you don't factor in the part where you quit your job, moved in with Mom, and left Sam just hanging out there."

"Is that payback for the comment I made about why you don't have any money, or because I agree that Malcolm should sit to pee if he wants to?" I ask.

"Both. We're even now," Marjorie says. "Is there anything I can do?"

"Stop by and visit her, maybe ask her to go out to lunch," I say.

"Oh, there are some good trunk shows coming up; maybe she'd like that," Marjorie says.

She gets out her personal organizer. It's Hermès. It's orange. She flips it open. Not a single square on the calendar is blank. What can't fit in the squares is in the margins, with arrows pointing toward a date. Opportunities on the sidelines.

"There's something at the Whitney on Tuesday. A thing at the Central Park Zoo on Wednesday. The ballet's annual Hawaiian Night is coming up!" Marjorie is visibly excited by this last realization. Actually shaking a bit in anticipation.

"Hawaiian Night?" I ask.

"So fun! We get to dance the hula and wear floral dresses!" Marjorie says.

"It sounds perfect," I say.

Nana

ONCE A MONTH I drive to the Short Hills Mall in New Jersey to visit my grandmother. Nana.

Nana is a mall walker. No map required. She uses landmarks to navigate. A shop that sells pink and blue eye shadow, tiaras, and faux Hope diamonds to nine-year-olds is her North Star.

"Join a gym," I say.

"Oh, piffle, why would I do that?" Nana says. "So I can be the old lady at the gym? No thank you."

"So I don't have to be related to a mall walker," I say.

"Stop being selfish and mind your own business," Nana says.

"Can we take a water break?" I ask.

"If we must," Nana says.

We take a seat at a coffee place. She knows a handful of mall-walking octogenarians who also use the mall as their adjunct gym/office.

"How's Joan?" Nana asks.

"Good," I say. "Hard to tell actually. One minute she's optimistic, then in denial, then just very, very busy doing nothing that matters."

"That's normal. To want to keep busy, to keep it out of your mind. My scare came at about her age," Nana says.

Her scare? What scare?

"You had cancer?" I say.

"Oh, sure," Nana says.

"I never knew that," I say.

Our family history is a never-ending surprise party.

"It was right after the divorce. You girls came to see me in the hospital. Your mother told you I had my tonsils removed," Nana says. "It seemed ridiculous, but she said she was trying to space out the awful news. Organizing, as usual."

"I don't know what to say. Really. I'm at a loss."

"Well, once you have it it's never off your radar again," she continues. "After six years you think about it less, after ten years, you take a deep breath. Feel lucky. At fifteen years you really start to think things might be okay. So far, so good. It's been almost twenty-five years."

"They've scheduled her lumpectomy. It's in a few weeks," I say. "Maybe you can call her, or go to the hospital."

"She'd hate that," Nana says. "We haven't spoken in years; she won't want me visiting her in a hospital when she's vulnerable."

"You're her *mother*. Aren't you supposed to call the shots?" I ask.

Magical Obsessions

SITTING ACROSS FROM PAUL, I stare into space. I mentally reshuffle the books on his bookshelves. Organize them by color of spine. Surprisingly few books have turquoise covers. They pop out at you. Then I reorganize them from tallest to shortest, also in my head.

"So, where are you right now?" Paul asks.

"Reorganizing your books again," I say. "It's strangely satisfying."

"Another magical obsession," Paul says.

"I wouldn't call it an obsession," I say. "Or magical."

"What would you call it?" Paul asks.

"I don't know," I say. "It's not important what you call it. You can call it an obsession if you want to."

"Thanks," Paul says.

I return to staring and reorganizing. I hope he doesn't interrupt again. Because if he does I'll have to start organizing the books all over. I notice individual reams of paper near his desk. Different brands. He's buying paper by the individual ream. Is he a Rockefeller or something?

"That's the most expensive way to buy paper, you realize," I say. "You should buy it by the case, it's half the price. Even less than half the price. You're throwing money away."

"Are you worried about my finances?" Paul asks.

"No," I say. "I don't know; maybe I'm just worried in general. Mostly I'm just sitting here wondering why on earth my mother didn't ever tell me that my grandmother had cancer, too. How could that not come up? My grandmother had cancer when she was my mother's age—that's not worth mentioning? Not worth tossing into a conversation somewhere along the line? The number of family secrets is just staggering."

"The surprise is that you continue to be surprised," Paul says.

Roommates

THERE OUGHT TO BE some kind of Hallmark holiday celebrating nurses and home-health-care workers. These people are living saints. I don't know how they do it.

My biggest challenge is getting my mother to sit still. She's been sneaking off to Bikram yoga classes. When she thinks I'm sleeping, she calls the New School on a daily basis to see if there's been any movement on the waitlist for the six-part sushi-making class.

According to Mom, her doctor recommended rest, relaxation, and meditation prior to surgery. I'm torn between wanting her to follow doctor's orders and wanting her to live her life.

We play hearts. She cheats when I go to the kitchen to get us water. She says she was joking, not cheating. We switch to Scrabble, which gets even more heated. Mom claims it's okay to use British spellings and Spanish words. Only if you're playing Scrabble in the U.K. or Mexico, I say. For the record, she's good at Scrabble. Crossword-puzzle people are always good at Scrabble.

Maybe we should paint or spend our time doing crafts. Anything that involves a less definitive outcome. Games with clear winners and losers aren't good for us. But instead of creative pursuits, we've taken the easy way out and turned on the TV.

We've started watching *The Passionate & the Youthful*. Daytime TV isn't just a guilty pleasure. It is crack cocaine. You try and break the habit.

We narrowed the search for "our show" based on start times. Mom has to be home at eleven A.M. to take her medications. She can't take them on an empty stomach, so we've begun our ritual of green tea, cookies, medication, and settling ourselves in front of the TV.

I never realized that soap operas largely revolve around hospitals. There is always the two-faced nurse, who wants to sleep with the hot and altruistic doctor, who spends his vacation fixing the cleft palates of orphans in South America. The former stripper turned nurse who fears her past will be revealed. Once a week a patient arriving at the ER threatens to ID her. There's always a foreign doctor self-medicating for reasons unknown, and a male nurse who has a suspicious number of elderly patients dying under his watchful "care."

I can speak with some authority when I say *The Passionate & the Youthful* is the best of the bunch, because we sampled them all for several days before settling on our favorite.

We found true happiness at the supermarket when Mom discovered *Soap Opera Weekly*. A magazine devoted to the on- and off-screen antics of daytime television celebrities. We had to buy two copies because we didn't want to share.

It's over pistachios and raspberry tea that I finally have the guts to say it.

"Mom, I'm not nurse material," I say.

"I don't need a nurse," Mom says. "I feel perfectly lovely."

"We should have had this conversation before I quit my job," I say.

"Don't get me wrong. I'm happy you're here. But I'm not the reason you quit that job," Mom says. "I have no idea why you turned out so afraid."

"I don't either," I say. It's half true.

My second-grade teacher's euphemism for a lie was "half truth." But it's not that straightforward. Like most big decisions, quitting my job was part of a chain reaction waiting for the perfect combination of events to set it off.

I wouldn't have quit my job if she had not been diagnosed. Yet she is not the reason I quit my job. She is the push that got me to quit the job, which I was all too happy to quit in the moment. It was a convenient time to escape getting closer to Sam. It also looked like I might have a helpful role in my mother's life. A closeness that was never there. I had a split second to choose at the fork in the road, and I chose the past instead of the future. I don't regret choosing the well-traveled road.

But to say she has no clue what I'm afraid of . . . As far as I know, my mom hasn't had a relationship that was important to her since my father disappeared. It's more than a little terrifying to be all she has.

Jim's Office

IT'S WINTER, and I walk the eighteen blocks to my father's office in new boots. I'm taking him up on his offer of lunch, which he made out of politeness that day at my mom's. He's rescheduled twice already. I'll be shocked if he's at work when I arrive.

Since I now must account for the time I spend away from my mother, I walk everywhere. It allows me to leave home twenty minutes early for each outing. Because when I'm not with her, that must mean there is something more important . . . some competition for my attention.

I show identification, then take the elevator to the twenty-ninth floor. The elevator seems to fly straight up in the air, and I feel taller when it stops. Above the little people. Height by association. I exit the elevator. There is a wide corridor leading to a large wooden desk, encased in bank-type bulletproof glass. It is the nucleus of this legal establishment. The stopgap. I'm guessing it's a post–9/11 installation. A moderately useful monument to over-the-top security measures.

A gray-haired woman sits behind the desk. She adjusts her glasses. She doesn't recognize me, so she waves me off with her hand and returns to her paperback.

I knock on the glass. She doesn't look up. I pace. I knock again. She ignores the knock. The perfect analogy for the relationship I have with my father. He's right there, around the corner, less than fifty feet away. And so un-reachable.

I knock on the glass again. The old woman shrugs. Points to the elevator. I point to her, and then to the door. I mouth the words "I'm here to meet Jim—Jim Rhode."

Someone else approaches the glass door. Raps his knuckles, and shakes the handle.

"Her vision isn't great," he says. "And she refuses to make coffee, but—"

"She's a good kisser?" I say.

"Well, that, too," he says. "But I was going to say that she bakes these amazing homemade pies every few weeks."

A loud dull buzz precedes a loud click, followed by the sound of vibrating glass. The freeing of the lock. He holds it for me. "Who are you here to see?" he asks.

"Jim Rhode," I say.

"Check fraud? Divorce? New will? Nothing violent, I hope," he says.

"Free lunch," I say. Avoiding my life. Breaking in some new shoes. The list could go on and on.

"I'm Will. That's Esther," he says, pointing to the coot behind the glass. "Don't get on her bad side," Will says.

Will looks young. Too young to be a lawyer. He should be at a frat house, doing rip cords.

"I'm Emily," I say, shaking his hand.

Will points me in the direction of Jim's office. I walk down the hallway. I knock.

"Come in," Jim says.

It is well lit. Clean, but messy. His desk is old. His bookcases are full. He has a crystal paperweight on his desk. A lion.

"Did you remember lunch?" I ask. "You said to meet you here."

"Yes," Jim says. "Yes, of course I remembered. How's your mother?"

"Good. Most of the time. She vacillates between 'Should I redecorate the co-op' to 'If I die, I want you to be in charge of who gets my eyes; give my other organs to anyone you want, but my eyes are special!'" I say. "An exchange student who lived with us in the early nineties is at the house helping her organize personal papers. It's good for her to feel like she's controlling someone."

"Yes, she always excelled at that. Glad to hear she has a project. She's always liked a project," Jim says. He reminds me of my mother when he says this.

"That's a unique take on cancer," I say. "A project . . ."

"Well, I was really talking about getting her personal papers in order, but I can see how you might have heard it that way," Jim says.

We walk out to the reception area.

"Who's the girl, Jim?" Esther asks.

"We met on the way in," I say. "I'm Emily."

She extends her hand to shake and surprises me by squeezing my hand as hard as she can, harnessing all of ninety-five pounds into that iron goddess grip.

"Ouch," I say. I pull my hand away from the Claw.

"Weren't expecting me to be so strong, were you?" Esther says.

No, I just wasn't expecting you to be so damn mean!

"Not really," I say.

We wait for the elevator, and then wave good-bye to Esther and the Plexiglas that protects her from the sneezes of strangers.

"What's her problem?" I ask.

"Oh, you know how some people have to prove themselves every single day of the week," Jim says. "I feel for her, I really do. But it's no excuse for stealing. We can't tolerate a thief here. The group is too small. It feels personal."

"What does she steal?" I ask.

"It started small. Pens. Paper. A few weeks ago she came in on a Sunday. Wheeled a bookcase right out of here. Security caught the whole thing on tape," Jim says.

"Wow, what did she say when you showed her the tape?" I asked.

"Oh, we haven't confronted her. We don't want to humiliate anyone; we just want her to move along and think it was her idea to leave," Jim says.

Jim takes a quick look at what I'm wearing.

"You're underdressed," Jim says.

"You never said where we were going," I say. "It's nothing new, though. I never have a clue where I'm going."

"It's okay," Jim says.

"It's going to have to be," I say.

I decide I need some talking points. Jim and I do not accomplish much when we talk. I'm half shocked that the mirage has a voice.

I make a mental list. Favorite color? Who cares? MAC or PC? Lefty or righty? Flat or sparkling? Now we're getting somewhere! In no particular order I start to list some of my favorite things. Getting a new CD, playing it over and over again for an entire weekend. Craving song 8, but not fast-forwarding to 8. Just waiting and enjoying the internal countdown. Driving go-karts. Kayaking. Baking cupcakes. Finding something I've lost. Reading a book I can't put down.

Leftover Love

WE'RE IN THE LARGE dining room at the Club. It overlooks the FDR and the East River. The river is always swirling and moving faster that you'd expect it to, making it a stressful backdrop for anyone who is paying attention. But no one seems to be paying attention to it, except for me.

We sit at his table. His usual table. What is it with everyone I know having his own table in a restaurant? Everyone except me? How long do you have to go to a restaurant to get your own table? How nice do you have to be? How much do you need to spend? Is your table for dinner also your table for lunch—and breakfast? Who do you lose your table to?

A man dressed in a green polyester uniform with brass and gold nautical detail takes our order. His name tag says MARTIN, but we have no need to know his name. It makes me think it's not his real name. It's just something he's adopted here, at the Club. For his role as a waiter. Name tag? You want me to wear a name tag? Okay, I'll wear *a* name tag. But not *my* name tag. Way to stick it to the man, "Martin."

"Martin, we'll have two chopped salads, two dirty martinis," Jim says.

"Great choice, sir," Martin says, not writing anything down. My father reaches for the basket on the table. He offers me some bread.

"Still at Schroeder, Sotos, Willett, and Ritchie?" Jim asks.

"No. Not really," I say. I had no idea he knew where I worked.

He puts some butter on his bread. I notice his watchband is old and the leather is cracking. His cuff links and shoes are polished, so I decide he likes the way the watchband looks. Worn. Trusted.

"Not really?" Jim says.

"I don't like being quoted," I say.

Martin brings our martinis. We sip them. I cough. Who knew people really drink martinis at lunch?

"Everyone likes being quoted. It feeds the ego," Jim says. "Who doesn't want to hear his own conversational highlights?"

"Maybe it's a gender thing," I say.

His words are matter-of-fact, but his tone is friendly, kind. He doesn't seem at all self-conscious that we are essentially strangers. Or if he is self-conscious, I don't know him well enough to read the signs.

"Where are you then?" Jim asks.

"Nowhere," I say. "I quit. I needed to take a break, and I thought Mom could use some support. But as usual, I forgot who I was dealing with. She's amazing. She's managed to turn breast cancer into a social network."

"Well, I can understand why you'd quit. I don't know why *anyone* would want to be a lawyer anyway," Jim says.

The relief of having someone say the right thing should never be underestimated, whether he means it or not.

"*You're* a lawyer," I say. "And you should have mentioned all this when I was applying to law school." My thankfulness wears off, the way thankfulness does.

"I don't think we were on speaking terms at the time," Jim says.

"Right," I say. "Well, then, you're forgiven for that one."

The salads are delivered. We start to eat. So this is what it's like to have a father?

"My father was a lawyer," Jim says, as if that justifies his life's work.

"Ironically, so is mine," I say. "I never met your father, did I?"

"No," Jim says. "And neither did I."

I don't remember his mother, either. I just remember that in her kitchen, she had a rack of wooden spoons, in graduated sizes. When I was about three, my grandmother showed me which spoon she used to hit my father with when he was "bad." I cried whenever we went to her apartment; I was terrified to go into the kitchen.

"So being a lawyer—is that your way of getting to know who your father was?" I ask. Clearly it's mine.

"What else was I going to do?" Jim says.

"It's a big world filled with commerce and art and possibility," I say.

"Art?" Jim says suspiciously, and dismissively. As if he is aware there is a thing called art, but wonders why I'm mentioning it to him.

"Yes," I say. "Art. Sculpture. Painting. Unique expression. Commentary on contemporary life—"

"I know what art is," Jim says.

Then why'd you put those dull lithographs all over your office? I want to say. But I know the answer. People want their lawyer's office to look responsible. It's reassurance that when the lawyer goes home at night, he's so steadfast, he works. He doesn't loosen his tie, or go out, or have a life. He's beige and boring and reliable. If you walked into a lawyer's office and he had a Warhol electric chair painting on his wall, you'd have some serious questions to ask.

"Contract law? What was I thinking? Why didn't I choose family law—like you? You're probably out of your office by six o'clock every night," I say. It's a relief to finally say it. To admit that I wasn't very thoughtful about a really important choice.

He thinks for a while.

"Have you considered turning this hiatus into something really special? How about backpacking through Europe. Not necessarily with a backpack, though. The human back is an underengineered thing. A really shoddy design, if you ask me. You could stay in some wonderful old hotels. The lake region of Italy is fabulous."

This is a response that perfectly describes my father. My mother's just been diagnosed with cancer, and feels so alone she begged me to move in with her. I've just thrown my job out the window, in theory to tend to her, and he suggests I run away to see some Italian lakes. Go off and see something beautiful and distant . . . How do you become so monumentally lacking in empathy? You practice every day until it sticks.

"You want me to spend six hundred dollars a night on a hotel room in Italy. I've just quit my job, and I bought a co-op last year. Shouldn't you be telling me to run to my boss and ask him for my job back? Network with other lawyers? I've thrown my entire life off course," I say.

"Maybe that's what you needed to do. I wish I'd done that," Jim says.

Silence. Is he being ironic?

"You *did* do that," I say.

"Yes. My only mistake there—and it was a big one—was timing," Jim says. "I should have done it earlier—before I was married. You still have time. Really, ask yourself: Do you *want* to be a lawyer?"

"Please tell me these aren't the motivational tactics you use on your employees," I say.

"It's not my responsibility to motivate them," Jim says.

"I don't want to be a lawyer to the exclusion of all other things—and sometimes that feels like what the choice is. All or nothing," I say. "But I'm not sure that I *never* want to be a lawyer."

"You get only one life," Jim says. "You could come work for me."

His non sequiturs sometimes sound like they may have come from inside of a fortune cookie.

"You're hiring more lawyers?" I ask, surprised by my own interest.

"Oh, no. We're chockful of lawyers. But you could become our receptionist when Esther 'retires.' It could very well change your life," Jim says.

"How would answering phones change my life?" I ask.

"You'll either have a new appreciation for contract law

or you'll discover that you enjoy having your evenings to yourself. It's a nice group of people we have working there," Jim says.

"So with one life—I should use it up on answering a phone? Buzzing people into your office?"

"The receptionists get to leave at five-thirty. You have to like that," Jim says.

"Do you happen to know how much you pay receptionists?" I ask.

"I have no idea," Jim says. "It can't be much. Next to nothing, I imagine."

"So they do it for the love of the game? Or is it the added perk of having all the free coffee and microwave popcorn they can enjoy?" I ask.

"It's amazing how that butter flavoring tastes so real," Jim says. "I resisted trying it for years. Big mistake. Of course, the office smells like a goddamn movie house."

"It really *does* taste like butter," I say. We have something in common! We both adore popcorn prepared in the microwave!

I stare for a while. How did the topic of what to do with the rest of my life turn into this? I can't quite figure out what to make of my father's suggestion that I go to Italy. Is the trip supposed to spare me the experience of my mother's cancer? Or does he just want me to be the one to leave this time? Ease his guilt?

We drain our martini glasses.

I make a joke about answering phones all day and

my official cause of death being listed as "bad case of boredom."

My father gets annoyed. He's not amused by any reference to the great good-bye. Despite the ravenous dating habits he enjoyed while married to my mother, it turns out he's quite sensitive about his ex-wife's diagnosis. Perhaps there is some leftover love between them. Or guilt. Sometimes love and guilt look the same.

"You are so much like your mother," Jim says.

"How would you know?" I ask.

He stares out the window.

There's nothing I can do about my mother's health. Crying hasn't helped. Neither has the career suicide or personal-life sabotage. But the dirty martinis have been tasty. For a few minutes there, I was enjoying getting to know my father. Until that last comment.

"Well, think about the job," Jim says.

"I already have," I say.

"And?" Jim says.

"I'll take it. Thanks," I say.

My inheritance is right here in the room with us, boiled down to a simple equation. My mother's fear of communicating married to my father's immaturity. It's all mine now! And I don't want any of it. What I add to this heap is longing. It's a romantic and useless notion, unless it's converted into something resembling personal satisfaction and a blueprint for happiness.

Love Map

MAPS, ALL OF THEM, hopefully imply there are places you should want to be, and people working diligently to make it easier for you to get there. I like to imagine a band of solitary travelers dispersed and making all the wrong turns so I don't have to. I long for the neat, personal map that warns me of the wrong turns that could have saved me the inconvenience of a few side trips in my life.

Steve was one such pit stop. He was cute, distant, and extremely cheap. Tight with money and love: Congratulations! You've arrived at your destination!

A map might also have prevented me from stumbling into Miller. In spite of the fact that he held on to a deep, deep hope that I'd agree to hurt him during sex, he made me laugh. In the morning, he'd serve me café latte in a china cup. Sans pants, but taking the time to don a cowboy hat, he'd teeter across the floor not spilling any coffee. He was a runner, and I'd watch him carry that latte cup away in amazement. Plus, he still seemed like such a kid, and in that way he was a relief. A temporary thing requiring no stressful tests to see how my past might repeat itself in my future with him.

A map might have warned me that my mother would be getting sick, and that my father would reappear. That he'd try to rewrite history, and that he'd be too late.

There are maps to places you have no right to go, like maps of the stars' homes. You've got no business driving by Siegfried and Roy's home on a Thursday afternoon—but still, you can. Facilitators of your wishes are practically daring you to go. Here is the map. A map is permission. Señor Siegfried won't mind.

Of course, our parents leave us maps—musty, folded the wrong way, and stowed in the glove box in case you need them. They were good enough for my parents; they must be good enough for me! Only problem is, I know where my parents ended up.

You could brace yourself for the various pileups along the way. Sixty miles 'til infidelity; watch out for the fork in the road at every family holiday; and whatever you do, don't mention how Dad falls asleep at "an old friend's" house "due to unforeseen weather," sickness, sprained ankle, thunderstorm, pants on fire . . . That's the sucker's map because it shows the easiest and most dangerous road to follow. And when you're not paying attention, just cruising along, searching for what's next, it can also be the most hypnotic and appealing. Don't ever underestimate the allure of what looks easy.

Psychologists say our "love maps" are established by the time we're seven years old. At seven, I loved trolls. I loved diaries. My father had become a stranger. My love map is really more like a set of sketchy directions scribbled on a cocktail napkin.

In the end, all of us will have created a map that works

only for us. If anyone else dared to follow it, he'd be signing up for a horrific triptych the likes of which the automobile club could never even conceive.

As for right now, I'm lost. A map, any map, would be greatly appreciated. I'm not the first lost person to feel this way. Lost people just want a way out; they'll follow any foolish trail.

Paul Molé

IT'S SATURDAY. We are weighted down with ski coats, mittens, and boots. We walk around the Central Park Reservoir. One of our daily rituals.

"You're not getting the full effect if you aren't landing on your heel and rolling up to the ball of your foot, and then off your toes, each time your foot lands," Mom says.

"You don't like the way I'm walking?" I ask.

"I took a walking class at Canyon Ranch," Mom says.

"A walking class?" I say.

"I enjoy these walks with you," Mom says.

"Me, too, we argue less when we're moving," I say.

"We don't argue. I have no idea where you get these ideas of yours," Mom says. "Listen, after this, let's go home, get showered, and then go over to Paul Molé."

"The barbershop?" I ask. I had all of my childhood haircuts there.

"I've decided I'm going to get my head shaved before

the surgery," Mom says. "I don't want any hospital intern cutting all of my hair off."

"First of all, it's too cold to shave your head. If you really want to do that, wait until the summer. Second, you aren't having chemotherapy; you aren't going to lose your hair. You're having a lumpectomy and then a few radiation treatments," I say.

"You're just saying that to make me feel good. Besides, I like the idea of getting my head shaved. It seems empowering," Mom says.

"On second thought, don't take my word for it, go get your head shaved," I say.

Mothers and Daughters

NANA AND I MEET at the mall. The stores open at ten. Management, very kindly, unlocks the doors to the main building for the loiterers at nine.

"Can we walk slow today? I'm not in the mood," I say.

"Oh, please," Nana says, not slowing down.

"I've taken a job," I say.

"Good. Wallowing is a waste of time," Nana says.

"We haven't been wallowing . . . we've been watching TV," I say. "And making smoothies. Do you think the antioxidant burst is negated by the vodka we dump in?"

"Whatever puts a smile on your face," Nana says.

"Good point," I say.

"I'm glad you're going back to work though. Your

mother can manage her own affairs. She always has," Nana says.

"It annoys me that you talk about your daughter that way," I say. "She's my mother, so I get to be as critical as I want to be. But I don't think you should be so critical of your daughter—especially now."

"It's the only real advantage to getting older. You get to say what you mean and stop apologizing," Nana says. "I'm not critical of your mother because I don't love her; I'm critical of your mother because when she makes a mistake, she can't own up to it. It's very immature, and it has stunted her growth."

"So why not be the bigger person? Forgive her for whatever started this whole standoff. Do you even remember why you're so angry with her?" I say.

"I'm not senile," Nana says.

"So what's the story?" I say.

"I honestly think that is something you and your mother should discuss," Nana says.

She's never said anything like this to me before. It must really be good. Or have something to do with me . . . ?

"Who's being immature now?" I say.

"You'll have to trust me on this," Nana says. "Let's hear more about the new job. What kind of work will you be doing?"

"Receptionist," I say.

"Interesting choice for a lawyer," Nana says.

"At Jim Rhode's law firm," I say.

She stops walking. She smiles. She starts walking again.

"You tell him I said hello," Nana says.

"Okay," I say.

Training Day

I'M TAKING A JOB from a senior citizen. How's that for an injection of pride?

Esther is nearly a foot shorter than I am. She's deaf in her left ear when it's convenient. She's also legally blind when it works to her advantage. But there's not a Danielle Steel title she hasn't read.

"What did they say?" Esther asks, in a hushed voice. "I can take it."

"Who?" I say.

"The powers that be!" Esther says.

We're both speaking English, and yet . . .

"What is your question?" I ask.

"Did they say they fired me? Because they didn't," Esther says.

"Oh," I say. "I think they said something about retiring. That you were retiring. Are you . . . retiring?"

"They're giving me a three-month paid leave. Then I have to find a new situation. Nobody has the stones to fire me," Esther says.

"I haven't even started working, and your new job at home already sounds better than mine," I say.

"You understand the basic idea of this position, I take it?" Esther says.

I've watched her closely for twenty minutes, and I think I'm getting it loud and clear.

"Yes, I think I do. Never make them think I'm more capable than I am," I say. "Don't go the extra inch. Don't raise anyone's expectations."

"Right. Because the next thing you know you're spending your Saturday picking up their dry cleaning; you're buying last-minute intimate garments for Valentine's Day, taking the subway to three different stores in search of a pink satin push-up bra in 34C," Esther says.

My heart sinks on this one. "Esther, did someone really send you out to buy bras for a . . . lady friend? That's really not appropriate," I say. "I think you should file a complaint."

"No! Of course no one sends me out for bras! Because I never let things get out of hand. I stay professional. I read my books, I make my phone calls, do my nails. I keep to myself," Esther says. "I'm just imagining what could happen to a people pleaser such as yourself."

"Oh, I see," I say. She hates me for taking her job. *I* hate me for taking her job.

"Okay, you're on your own," Esther says. "Should someone ask, I'm in personnel, taking care of some paperwork."

"What if someone from personnel asks?" I say.

"Always keep the lie simple," Esther says.

"I thought you were going to train me all day," I say.

Keep the lie simple? I could actually learn things from this woman.

"You're a natural; I can tell," Esther says, fishing for a pack of cigarettes in her enormous leather bag. A gaggle of key chains dangle from her other hand, hypnotizing me. Must answer phones. Must answer phones.

Wrapping Paper

I SIT ON the floor looking through some of the photo albums Mom has assembled during the past few days. I haven't seen a single photo of me yet. Mostly they are beauty shots of her near other beautiful things. The Great Pyramid. The Eiffel Tower. Various beaches. Red hibiscus in hair posing somewhere in Los Angeles. She traveled with "friends," who I suspect she was kissing and keeping at arm's length. Close enough, but never too close. I was rarely introduced to them.

"Dad thought I should go to Italy," I say. He seems like a safe topic to bring up, now, since she's the one who brought him back into the fold. Does the mention of him flood her with memories, both good and bad?

"*He* should go to Italy," Mom says.

"He was probably hoping I'd suggest that," I say. "Or offer him some miles. But—just guessing here—was that what it was like to be married to him?"

"In a way," Mom says. "It wasn't all bad. But his head

was somewhere else, in the clouds. Things are different now. They treat people like him."

"People like him?" I ask.

"Depression. They treat it now," Mom says.

I didn't know he was depressed. The family details are given on a need-to-know basis. The everyday events of their lives are such close-held secrets that a stranger might think their dealings had the commonly recognized value of gold and must be guarded. Instead, each detail is held in reserve for when my mother is ready to share what she considers to be ancient history and insignificant.

"You never mentioned that before," I say.

"You never asked," Mom says.

"How can you say that with a straight face?" I ask, annoyed. "I was young when he left. There are hundreds of details I don't remember. I don't remember what it was like to have him around. I don't remember if we ate breakfast together every morning. I don't remember celebrating birthdays. I don't remember any of it. Shall I start firing off random questions and hope some land near the mark? 'You never asked'? You're infuriating!"

"That's sad," Mom says. "Really—it's sad. I'm sorry you don't remember him. But I was focused on raising my two children. There wasn't time for me to offer color commentary."

I reject the urge to slap her. I'm stronger than I would have guessed.

"Stop making it sound like I'm being unreasonable. We had a father one day, and poof, the next day he was gone," I say. "You didn't seem to miss him for a second. Marjorie and I were devastated. That's a bizarre disconnect for an *adult* to understand. We were only children!"

"I cried at night in my room," Mom says, "so you girls wouldn't see."

"Maybe that was a mistake," I say. "All I thought was that if Dad disappeared, you could too."

"I'd never disappear!" Mom says. "Besides, *Marjorie* seems fine, now."

I know she believes that, I'm just shocked she actually said what she believes.

"I'm sorry, that didn't come out right," Mom says. "You seem fine, too. You wait here. I'll be right back."

My sister Marjorie does seem fine, if your definition of fine is someone who can't balance a checkbook and has a serious obsession with shopping for things she does not need. She also has no interest in having a relationship with her partial clone, our mother. My mother thinks that's *normal* because she has no interest in having a relationship with her mother.

Mom walks into one of the guest rooms and opens the closet doors. I hear digging. She returns with a box that is beautifully wrapped.

"I have a present for you," Mom says.

The week my father left we shopped. That I remember.

We got new clothing. Marjorie and I got matching plaid spring jackets and new white sneakers. We got new toys: Shrinky Dinks; Sea-Monkeys; an art case filled with markers, paints, and pastels. We were full of things and preoccupations, and empty of emotion.

Mom thrusts the gift toward me and smiles. She's taken to giving me gifts on a regular basis now. She is working on the assumption that she could miss many Christmases and birthdays. Valentine's Days. Easters. Is it a feeling that will fade with time like Nana described?

I hate this gift idea for so many reasons. I hate her fear of being deprived of future holidays. And here's where my great selfishness simply cannot hide itself: I'm hoping one of the gifts she gives me might indicate that she really knows me, and knows what I might like to receive.

The wrapping paper is beautiful.

"I bought the paper at the Met," Mom says. "Years ago. No point in saving it, right? You should use the nice things in life."

She wears all of her jewelry now, too. She doesn't "save the good stuff" for special occasions. Sometimes she wears too much of it at once. Still, it seems like a giant step forward for her. Not waiting, just doing.

She's apparently stockpiled gift wrap from a host of museums up and down the eastern seaboard, because each time I open a gift, it's wrapped in "special" paper she's been saving. The paper is always more wonderful and elaborate than the gifts, which range from unusual, to bizarre, to insulting.

I open the box and inside is a misshapen top. Large and bright blue.

"I know you love blue," Mom says, a huge smile on her face.

Actually I don't love blue. Not royal blue, anyway. I like periwinkle, and I'm a small-medium, not a shapeless-large.

"Are these walruses?" I ask, even though they are clearly walruses.

"Cute, don't you think?" Mom says.

"Thank you," I say. "Thank you for the gift, Mom."

"You are so very welcome!" Mom says. "The kids will love it!"

Long silent pause while I figure out what to do with this comment.

"Kids?" I ask.

"Your children," Mom says, pretending to be bewildered.

I sit in silence. This time I can't quite take it.

"I don't understand why you say things like that. 'The kids will love it!' I don't have children," I say. "You know I don't have children, I'm not married; I don't have a boyfriend—"

"Oh, but you will!" Mom says. "I may not be around for it, but you will. They'll be lovely children."

More silence.

I slip the walruses over my head. The shirt swims on me. But I need to put it on to punctuate the insanity of this "gift." Her smile fades a bit. The walruses have iridescent glitter on their tusks. There are surprises around every corner. Someone designed this. But it didn't feel "finished" until the glitter was added to the tusks. And then, ah, perfection.

"Couldn't you just once buy me a gift for who I am *now*?" I say. "One time?"

She looks at me, and I know what she's thinking. How ungrateful. I have a mother who *survived*, and all I can do is complain about this shirt. This fun shirt she bought for me. Sure it needs to be tailored, but still, it's fun.

What she fails to take into account is that she herself would never wear walruses—regardless whether her child would have "loved" this shirt. She wouldn't risk being ridiculous for anyone.

Her feelings are hurt. She goes off to take a nap. She runs away.

Coping Skills

THERE IS A KNOCK at our front door, and then it opens. Perry walks in. He's wearing jeans. Sunglasses and a linen shirt.

"Hey, my gay bowling league ran late. Sorry," Perry says.

Perry and I went to high school together. After school,

we'd drink beer, and he'd try on my mother's jewelry and tummy-control undergarments.

I lived with my mother. He lived with his father. We brought unique perspectives into our relationship. It did occur to me that he was using me to get to my mother's girdles, but I liked him too much to care.

He drops a box of wine to the floor, hands my mother some daffodils, and gives her a big hug.

"Oh, Perry, thanks for the flowers. Careful, that's a linen shirt I'm wearing," Mom says.

Perry was about to break the hug until my mom made the comment about the shirt. Then he decided to hug longer. Wrinkle her shirt more.

"Enough hugging," Mom says, trying to pull away.

"Oh, come on," Perry says. "I know you have a steamer in this place somewhere."

Mom breaks away and carries the flowers into the kitchen.

"Cute shirt," Perry says. "A Nana hand-me-down?"

"Should we take the wine into my bedroom?" I ask.

"Sure," Perry says.

As a teenager, Perry was the only boy allowed in my bedroom.

I sit on the floor. Perry stretches out on the bed.

"I'm starting to think that what you need are some coping skills," Perry says with authority. "You have no model to follow. No instructions on how to get through the shit end of things."

The way he says it makes it sound so attainable. Like I can walk into a store, pick up a bag of coping skills, go home, and slip them on. One size fits all. Bing-bang. And we're on to the next problem.

I'll just leap over these hurdles of illness, relationships, and unemployment and land on the other side happy and complete.

If you'd told me a month ago that I'd be drinking wine out of a box and sharing my problems with Perry, I'd have thought that sounded too good to be true. If you'd told me that two years ago, it would have depressed me to no end.

We met in drama club. I worked on scenery and wanted to be respected. He directed the school plays and wanted to be loved. I was on the shy side, so I latched onto people who talked a lot. If I chose well, very little was required of me.

After an hour of catching up and drinking, the wine is starting to make me woozy. My mind is drifting.

"What are you thinking about?" Perry says.

"Ask again later," I say.

"Ah, your favorite answer," Perry says.

That first day at my mother's, when she was asleep on the davenport and I was in her bedroom trying on her lipstick, some part of me wanted her to die. Her death would be over, and I could stop imagining where I'd be when I get the news; or worse, that I'd watch her die. I can't say that even to Perry. It's so horrible to want to fast-forward through anyone's life—or death. Skip the grief and jump to the next scene. Skipping the grief is an eerie U-turn back to childhood.

My grief is so old it's a habit. It is so much a part of me that I'm afraid to give it up. My father left, and, until tonight, no one spoke about it. His return mainly leaves me curious about his departure and his attempt at a reunion. My mother's cancer reminds me only of what I didn't experience while it was happening. I wasn't allowed to.

I have this unrealistic view of things. I believe life should be a series of seamless transitions. When it's not, I'm shocked and disappointed. My mother cried in her room, alone, hiding all of those transitions.

"Do you ever feel like you'll never be ready for a healthy relationship until you resolve your relationship with your parents?" I say.

"I had a healthy relationship. I'm not sure I want another one," Perry says.

It's been nearly a year since Perry's boyfriend Roger died. He never talks about him.

"Sometimes you just need to plow forward," I say.

"Listen to you," Perry says.

Who needs a map when there's only one passable road to the future? When you're headed in the only direction that makes any sense at all to you? You don't need a map to find your home.

Life is a selfish pursuit. You tend to your own little

corner of the world and hope your conscience keeps you in check. The first week after my mother was diagnosed, I felt guilty for reading the newspaper. Shouldn't that thirty minutes have been invested in a cure for cancer?

Vogue

NOT UNLIKE MANY WOMEN my age, I have begun praying as a result of an article in *Vogue*. Among the shoes and frocks of the fall season was a not-so-short article about the healing effects of prayer. Prayer is good—that was the gist of it—whether the person being prayed for knows he is being prayed for or not.

Now I pray for my mother while I'm on the treadmill at the gym. I pray for my mother while I'm at the bank machine, waiting for cash and a receipt. I changed my PIN to H-E-A-L. Empty seconds and minutes are now replaced with praying, and some begging, too. I pray for my mother before I go to bed. I pray whenever I think of it, which is often. And because I was raised with so little faith, I give God my address when I pray. It's a big world. A zip code, at the very least, has to be appreciated by the One in charge. The organized get rewarded.

After so much hard work, my heart races when I read a follow-up study that finds that praying for people may actually add undue pressure to them during recovery. They may heal more slowly and have more complications, perhaps out of the awesome responsibility to get well soon.

I continue to pray in my quiet, covert way.

Amnesty

I HAVEN'T BEEN back to my apartment in a week. Or maybe longer. Nothing inside has changed, which is a relief.

I sift through the mail. Con Ed bill. Cable bill. Reminder from the dentist. Two party invitations. One birth announcement. One letter. I love letters. Return address is East Sixty-second Street. The color of the paper is ecru, heavy bond. All male. I know what it says. The sentiment of it. He's disappointed in me. I've disappointed him. I'm a disappointment.

Dear Emily,

Did it really happen the way I remember it happening? You ran out of my office in midsentence? I also remember that you really like me. You like me way too much to end things like this.

I hope your mother is doing well. Let's talk when the time is right.

Regards, Sam

P.S. We're offering you amnesty regarding that stapler you "borrowed."

Okay, it turns out that's not what I thought it would say. . . .

Green

AT LEAST I'VE CAUGHT up on my magazine reading at these doctor appointments. You never know what you're missing until you have eight to ten hours to devote to magazines. You stumble across facts that surprise you, and you promise yourself you'll remember them. But there are gems on every page! It's not possible to retain all of this unnecessary information.

I've just read an article on interior design and choosing a paint color not to match your current mood, but to match the mood you want to *adopt.*

The walls of the hospital are painted pale green on purpose. It's supposed to soothe people. Calm them. Regulate their blood pressure.

Purple energizes. It's a good color for a gym, or a dance club. Orange is the color favored by the criminally insane.

My mother is in a pale green room changing into her hospital gown. And the doctor is in his pale green gown. His body fading into the pale green walls creates this bizarre effect of a disembodied head chatting me up. It's so distracting, it's impossible for me to listen carefully to what he's saying.

Yet he has the nicest voice in the whole world. People

must fall in love with him all the time. Not hero worship, either. He deals with cancer every day, and he knows that the people who are diagnosed do not. He's not tired of questions. He's not tired of explaining.

The Passionate & the Youthful is really making a mistake by not toning down Dr. Cleft Palate and modeling that character after Dr. Kealy instead. He's the kind of guy who would easily inspire fan clubs and major merchandising agreements.

More than anything, though, I finally feel that my mother is in good caring hands. A part of me realizes I need this fantasy. I need to believe that *someone* is stronger than the cancer and knows how to get rid of it.

"I'm sorry, I wasn't listening," I say.

"To which part," Dr. Kealy says.

"All of it, or, none of it," I say. "I was just thinking you've really been so nice, and that's made all the difference to me and to my mom. Really. Thank you."

"You're welcome," Dr. Kealy says. "Your mother is feisty. That's good. It will serve her well. I'm very optimistic. But this is serious surgery. We shouldn't be in there too long, maybe an hour or less. You can go sit with her until we're ready."

"Okay," I say.

It's so well organized. They do this every day, I tell myself. If you're going to get cancer, this is where you want to be.

I walk in the room. She's lying in the bed.

———

"HEY, DR. KEALY SAYS it won't take too long, and you can probably go home tonight," I say.

This will be the last conversation I have with my mother before she goes in for the lumpectomy. It is the closest I may ever come to knowing her. This strikes me as the conversation is happening. I know this is a window—a space in time that won't be duplicated. Perhaps she's been more vulnerable or frightened in her life, but in this room, in this gown, with this IV in her arm—she can't conceal it or walk away from it. Jokes don't work.

A clear plastic tube hangs down from her wrist. It runs up to a bag of liquid. There is blood on her hand from where they missed a vein—or two. There is a streak of brightly colored blood on the sheet, too. I roll it under, in hopes that she doesn't see it.

She reaches out for my hand.

"When you were born, you were a fussy one," Mom says. "Oh, you screamed and cried until your father held you."

I smiled at the recollection, which is not actually a recollection at all but a created memory. A story I'd been told so often when I was very young that I remember it as if it happened a week ago.

"Some babies are just that way; they have a preference. Your father always said it was because he talked to you so much when you were in the womb. He read to you.

Performed for you, really. I mean, when he told a story he was dramatic, animated. I was busy sewing. Getting things ready. I didn't talk to you until you were born. And by then it was too late; you already preferred him. You were his little girl."

In twenty-five years, the topic of my father never came up. Until now, we've observed a code of silence. We weren't just avoiding talking about him, it was deeper than that: he didn't exist. He was as absent from thought and conversation as he was from our lives. But now there is a certain longing in her voice.

"That's just not true," I say. But the tears were already in my eyes. It is something I've always felt guilty about; I never needed her that much, not the way mothers need their children to need them.

"Now," Mom swallows hard, trying not to cry, "now I can't help wondering if you didn't like me to breast-feed you because, I don't know, it was almost like you knew something was wrong. That something in me was poisonous. I think maybe babies know those things."

A few tears run down her cheek. I reach for a tissue, but she's already unrolled the sheet with the blood on it. She is about to dab her eyes when she sees the blood. I hand her some tissues, and reroll the sheet.

"How'd you like to be responsible for all of the laundry in this place?" Mom says, with a laugh.

As she's lying there waiting for surgery, I imagine a cancerous Pac-Man—or Lady Pac-Man—running through her body eating up her healthy tissue, her life, expanding its mass and taking over. Devouring the flesh that nurtured me, or longed to. I want to scream. And I'm mad that I'm of a generation that can best relate a parent's cancer to a video game.

Pay Phone

AN HOUR HAS COME and gone. I drink some tea. I look inside my wallet for some quarters.

I walk down the hall to a pay phone and call Sam.

"Hello?" Sam says.

"Hi," I say. "It's me. Emily."

"Hi. Where are you?" Sam asks. "A friend is here for brunch. Can I call you back?"

Still there and having brunch? Or has just come over to have brunch? Either way, it doesn't sound good.

"No. I'm at a pay phone at the hospital," I say. "I got your note."

"Good. How is it going with your mom?" Sam asks.

"She's in surgery right now, and it was supposed to take an hour . . . but it's been almost two hours. I'll let you go," I say.

"No, don't do that, I can talk," Sam says.

"I used all of my quarters," I say. "We can talk later. I mean, we should talk later."

"Let me know how things go," Sam says.

"Okay," I say.

Brunch. A friend. They seem like a distant luxury right now. In the fantasy version of this, Sam leaves his guests at his apartment and races to the hospital to be by my side. He is toting a honey-colored wicker picnic basket. It's lined in a lovely toile pattern. No, too girlie. It's lined in plaid. A handsome, manly plaid. Inside are assorted cheeses and fresh fruit and real china plates and silverware. Cloth napkins. The works. When Mom wakes, I'd introduce her to Sam. She'd make some comment about what a refined man he is—owning his own picnic basket and all. And everything would be okay.

But the reality is, he's moved on to brunch and regular life. He's not a dweller. His wife left him, and he didn't wallow. He lived his life. It's healthy. But it scares me. If he can move on from marriage and divorce, he can move on from the on-again, off-again relationship we had.

I call Marjorie.

"Hey," I say.

"How is she?" Marjorie asks.

"It's taking longer than it's supposed to," I say. "I'm feeling kind of panicky."

"Do you want me to come there and keep you company?" Marjorie asks. "You know I think hospitals are disgusting. They are filled with germs and people coughing. But I'll come over if you want me to. I really think she's going to be okay. Mom's tough. Dr. Kealy does that operation a few times a day."

ASK AGAIN LATER • 111

I start to imagine the torture of spending any time with Marjorie in a "disgusting" hospital. The price is too high.

"Oh, wait, I forgot. I have a cooking class with Marcella Hazan," Marjorie says. "She's the god of Italian cooking. Impossible to get into her class. I can't miss it. If you miss one, she bans you for life."

"That's the only kind of cooking class you'd ever take. But please, send flowers or something. I just needed to talk to someone. Everything will be fine, and I'll call you after I see her," I say. "By the way, thanks for that rant about dirty hospitals. Now I feel like I need to burn my clothing when I get home."

I think Marjorie is right. Everything will be fine. But sitting here alone makes me feel like I don't have a family. I'm lonely and helpless all at once.

I see now how useful some of my mother's traits are. If she were here, waiting to see me, she'd be dialing through her archival phone books. She'd elicit sympathy from strangers. She would not go uncomforted.

I dial the phone.

"Hello?" Jim says.

"Hi. It's Emily. What are you doing?" I say.

"Jumping on a trampoline," Jim says.

"Yeah, me, too," I say.

"Good for the heart," Jim says.

"Want to come and have coffee at the hospital?" I ask.

"The surgery was today?" Jim asks.

"Yeah," I say. "It's taking a long time, though, and I keep thinking she's going to die. That's crazy, right? It's a simple procedure. One lump."

"Your mother wouldn't die there; she doesn't like hospitals. Thinks they're dirty. Besides, dying in a hospital is convenient. Expected. That's just not her," Jim says.

Games

MY FATHER AND I drink coffee in the waiting room.

"I kind of wish I smoked at a time like this," I say.

"Me, too," Jim says.

We stare at the floor for a while. There is a TV hanging in the corner. Some people are watching *The Price Is Right.* How does Bob Barker do it? How does he play the same game every day for thirty years and still manage to smile and remember people's names and appear interested?

My father looks up. "I'm going on a trip. The first thing I'm going to pack in my suitcase is a bowling ball," Jim says.

I stare at him blankly. Did he just have a stroke? Is that what I'm witnessing?

"Now it's your turn," Jim says.

"My turn?" I ask.

"What are you putting in the suitcase?" Jim asks.

I sip my coffee.

"What suitcase?" I say. Do I need to have him admitted now? Or do I wait to see if things right themselves? I pray they do. I really can't see myself bouncing back and forth between oncology and whatever the stroke wing is called.

"You don't remember this?" Jim says. "We used to play it on car trips. It's your turn to put something in the suitcase. Then you have to say what I put in the suitcase and so on. . . ."

I have no memory of this game. I have no memory of road trips. He could be making this up, and I wouldn't know the difference.

"A bowling ball and . . . a number two pencil," I say.

"A bowling ball, a number two pencil, and an anemone," Jim says.

"Oh, I see. That's how you want to play it? Okay. A bowling ball, a number two pencil, an anemone, and a hot shoe," I say. "I'm taking you down, old man."

I regret the last part after I say it, because I said it in a way that could have been taken seriously. When I was actually grateful to have someone there with me.

"A bowling ball, a number two pencil, an anemone, and a hot shoe—what is a hot shoe?" Jim asks.

"It's a groove on a camera that holds the flash attachment," I say.

"I'll take your word for it—under protest," Jim says.

My plan is working. He protests. He forgets the order

of the words. Victory is closer than anticipated. In this moment life is simple.

"Oh, and you see people putting anemones in suitcases on a regular basis," I say.

"It's not a literal game," Jim says. "A bowling ball, a number two pencil, an anemone, a hot shoe—under protest—and a tension column," Jim says.

"A bowling ball, number two pencil, an anemone, a hot shoe—under protest—a tension column, and a carbon-iferous reptile," I say.

"Good one," Jim says.

Dr. Kealy is walking toward us. I wave. I get up from the waiting area and walk toward him. Jim is still talking.

"Bowling ball, number two pencil, anemone, hot shoe, tension column, carboniferous reptile, and hydraulic brake hose," Jim says.

"To be continued," I say.

"Things are looking great," Dr. Kealy says. "It went very well. We don't see any reason she shouldn't make a full recovery. All very textbook. She's sleeping now, but you can see her as soon as she wakes up."

The fear I had just a few hours ago when the surgery seemed to drag on is already becoming a distant memory. It's replaced by relief and gratitude and the way things used to be.

"Since everything's okay, I'll take off and let you have

your time with your mom," Jim says. He throws away his coffee cup and makes his way to the door. He waves.

"See you Monday morning," Jim calls.

"Thanks for keeping me company," I say.

"Of course," Jim says. "Tell your mom I said hello."

Neat Little Mass

"THE CANCER DIDN'T spread. Neat little mass," Dr. Kealy continues, still standing in the hallway. "As a precaution we'll follow up with radiation twice a week for two weeks."

"Neat little mass. She'll love that description! How long before she wakes up?" I ask.

"There was an issue with the anesthesia. She had an allergic reaction, so we had to give her more fluid and change the type of anesthesia we were using. So she's a little bloated, and she has a rash."

"But everything's okay? Can she still go home tonight?" I ask.

"Everything is okay, but she'll have to wait until tomorrow. We just want to watch her for a few more hours," he replies.

Everything is okay, except the part where it took twice as long as it was supposed to. And my mind started to imagine all of the horrible things that could have happened.

"Great," I say. "Thank you so much."

He starts to walk away.

"Excuse me," I call to him. "Who's going to explain the bloating part to her? I'm not sure I want to be in the room when that happens."

He laughs and keeps walking. His work is done. He's off to the next patient. Really, it's not funny.

I walk into her room. She's already out of bed studying her face in the mirror.

"I didn't see anything in the presurgical waiver about a fifteen-pound weight gain in the face," Mom says.

"You look fine. The swelling will go away quickly," I say. "Dr. Kealy said it couldn't have gone better. He said it was a neat little mass, and he got it all."

My mom is silent. I stop to appreciate the rarity of the moment. Then I look at her. Tears are streaming down her face.

"Honestly, Mom, it's just an allergic reaction," I say.

"It's not that," Mom says, crying again. "I'm so relieved to have that thing out of me. I hated knowing it was there."

My mom wipes her tears and starts making the bed.

"Why are you making the bed?" I ask.

"A room just looks so much nicer when the bed is made," Mom says. "Even this room."

"Hello?" I hear a familiar voice in the hallway. My mother looks shocked.

"Hello?" I hear Nana's voice again. She walks into the room. "Joanie, is that you?"

"No, Joanie checked out twenty minutes ago," my mother says. Then her face changes. For the first time in weeks she looks relieved. She takes her mother's hand. "I was just thinking about you. I really was."

"Oh, Joanie," Nana says. She studies her face. "You need to reduce."

My mother laughs. She doesn't let go of Nana's hand.

On the windowsill is a flowering plant and two vases of fresh-cut flowers.

"Who sent the flowers?" I ask.

"The plant is from Marjorie. The tulips are from Mavis," Mom says. "I feel terrible she's spending her money on me."

"You have cancer . . . she's known you for thirty years. It's okay for her to spend her money on you," I say. "Who are the other ones from?"

"A friend," Mom says.

"Which friend?" I ask.

A nurse comes in to go over post-operative procedures. No heavy lifting. No making any important decisions for forty-eight hours. She's nothing like the stripper on *The Passionate & the Youthful*.

The Facts

I PAY SOMEONE to listen to me. That someone is Paul. It was a big stumbling block standing between me and therapy. I am a good listener. Would I be a better listener if someone paid me? Maybe. Probably not for the long haul, though. I'd pay attention, then start to lose patience as soon as my insights didn't lead to changes in behavior.

In the real world, I don't like it when someone tells me something about myself that I haven't yet realized. If I lack the courage to tell myself something revealing, I'm not ready to hear it from someone else.

"How did you know," I ask, "that she's very treatable . . . that she wasn't dying?"

Paul uncrosses his legs, shifts his weight, and crosses his legs again. It's a stall tactic of his. Since upping my sessions to twice a week, I've realized it's what he does when he's deciding if he'll tell me the truth, or wait and see if I'll figure it out on my own.

"I don't remember saying that," Paul says.

"You didn't," I say. "Not really. You said I should talk to her doctor, but the way you said it made me think you didn't believe she was dying."

"From everything you've told me, your mother is a real . . . storyteller. She's entertaining, but she's rarely accurate," Paul says. "Why were you so willing to believe she was dying?"

"If I imagined myself in her situation, and I received her diagnosis, I could very easily convince myself I was dying," I say.

"Only because you're empathetic and you've been conditioned to assume the worst-case scenario," Paul says. "Most often the worst-case scenario doesn't happen."

"She couldn't imagine a positive outcome," I say. "I can relate to that."

"See, that's really useful," Paul says.

I don't like the way he says it, though. As if her cancer is helpful. Or a tool for us to use. It's not. It's something awful she has to go through. We're vultures waiting to take what might be useful.

"Why is she like that?" I ask.

"We can't know that without her sitting in this room with us. We can only learn about why you respond the way you do," Paul says.

"I really didn't like the way you said that—that this is all really valuable. It sounded really selfish," I say. "And kind of mean."

"What we're doing here is selfish. Or it's supposed to be. There's no other way to approach this," Paul says. "Wouldn't it be far worse if she were to go through this experience and nothing was gained?"

Somewhere inside of me, that's what I've thought all along, of course. That nothing would change between us, there would be no gain. That the opportunity got away—again.

"While we're being honest," I say, because revenge will be mine for his calling my mother a liar before I had the chance, "where's your wedding ring? Did you get divorced?"

"Why would you think I got divorced?" Paul says.

"No wedding ring," I say.

"When did you notice that?" Paul asks.

"I don't know, a few weeks ago. But when did you get divorced?" I ask again.

"I'm interested in why I must be divorced if I'm not wearing a ring," Paul says.

"So you're not going to tell me if you're divorced or not?" I ask.

"Not until we explore what this means to you, and what your fantasies about this are," Paul says.

"*So* annoying . . ." I say.

"What?" Paul says.

"I've been seeing you once a week—or more—for two years," I say. "You think it's not appropriate that I'd ask about why you aren't wearing your ring?"

"I didn't say it wasn't appropriate. I think it might be useful to ask about why you have leapt to the divorce conclusion?" Paul says.

"If your wife died, I think you might have taken a few personal days. If not, you'd be a heartless bastard, which you're not. If you'd lost your ring, you'd have a new one by now. That leaves divorce. There are other things, too. You've made your office look nicer; you were kind of forgetful for a month or two, that must have been when it happened," I say.

"What if I wasn't wearing a ring when you first met me? How would you feel? Would you feel safer if I weren't wearing a ring, or if I were wearing a ring," Paul says.

"Are you telling me you've been tricking me into

thinking you're married for the past two years?" I say. "There's something wrong with you."

"I'm not telling you anything," Paul says.

"Well, at least you're being honest now!" I say.

Recuperating

WE WATCH MOVIES. Play Scrabble. Then Bogle. The list of games we can play without getting into a standoff continues to dwindle. We seek other forms of tame amusement.

We shop for the world's most beautiful note cards at Kate's Paperie. We buy an assortment of colored pens and carefully match the ink to the envelopes. Then we write over-the-top thank-yous as both chore and entertainment. "Your amazingly fragrant and generous gift of flowers arrived at the perfect juncture . . . not only was the bouquet splendid and cheerful, the vase was beyond stunning! An heirloom in the making!"

Mom waits on her davenport, watching a movie, while I wait in line at the post office for forty-five minutes to buy an assortment of unique and limited stamps.

My mother counts her towels. She likes perfect sets of six or eight. If she has only seven towels, she donates them to charity and starts all over again with a new set.

"Why not buy one to match the others?" I ask.

"They won't match. All of that washing fades them," Mom says.

"They're white," I say.

"They discolor with time, and the manufacturer changes their decorative weave on purpose so new towels don't match old towels," Mom says. Another conspiracy revealed.

"What are you going to do when Dr. Kealy tells you that the tissue analysis has come back and everything is great, and that the cancer is really gone?" I ask.

"I can't think about that yet," Mom says.

That's what I thought.

Relaxing with Phil

I OPEN THE front door to my mother's apartment.

"I'm home," I say.

My mother is not in the living room. I walk into the kitchen. There's music coming from the kitchen. A man is wearing an apron and opening a bottle of wine. Mom's favorite macrobiotic cookbook is open, next to the stove. Candles are lit in the dining room.

"Hi, I'm Phil," Phil says.

"Hi, Phil. I'm Emily," I say. "Where's Joanie?"

"In the shower," Phil says.

"Oh. So how do you know Mom?" I ask.

"The relaxation workshop at the hospital," Phil says.

"She really enjoys that," I say.

My mom walks into the kitchen. "I thought you were having dinner with your father tonight," Mom says.

"I am," I say. "I thought I'd stop by to see if you needed anything. Sorry about dropping in. I'll see you later."

"How about tomorrow?" Mom says. "You might enjoy staying in your own place tonight."

"Sure," I say.

Unconscious Dating

I'M ABSORBED IN pushing back my cuticles. It's like they are the front line of an army that needs to be bullied into retreat on a regular basis. Did I push back my cuticles when I was a lawyer? No time! Now, well, they run when they see me coming.

My father is out of the office today. I'm left with no one to spy on. I look in my top drawer for materials to amuse myself while I wait for the phone to ring. An article in the *Observer* grabs my attention. The headline is "Freudian Matchmaker."

The story is about a new dating service. The unattached see a shrink, and the shrink sets them up with other pre-screened "patients." The theory being that the mental health professional has a better chance of setting up a suitable couple than two individuals using their own dim-witted judgment. This sounds perfectly logical to me. I want some of this psycho-romantique.

Mankind has veered off course in terms of lifelong mating. Historically speaking, marriages were more successful when partners were chosen for us, when freedom of choice was not yet part of the equation. And if it fails, it's not a personal failure—it's a trained professional's failure. Much easier on the ego.

I call and try to set up an appointment. They ask what my occupation is. I say, "Receptionist, but not really. I'm a lawyer . . . not really that either. I mean, I graduated from law school, but I'm a receptionist, for now."

Will is waiting to be buzzed back into the office. I push the button. Door opens.

"Well, which one is it? Are you a lawyer? Or a receptionist?" the woman says. "We don't have time to monkey around." It wasn't clear if "we" meant she and I were in cahoots and we needed to crack this code and quick; or if the "we" meant she had people with real jobs to assist, and if I wanted to be one of them, great. If not, hang up. Now! Also, I sense her use of "monkey around" is her going off script when she's supposed to remain professional. I don't appreciate that, but I get a rush when I realize this faceless person is not unflappable. And all this careful attention to a thirty-second phone call means I need to get a handle on the obsessive compulsive habits I've been perfecting.

Will, the cutest, youngest thing in this office, is listening to my conversation. He looks at the newspaper article I was reading. He stands behind my desk and starts massaging my shoulders.

I turn and look at him and mouth the words "What are you doing?" Will smiles.

"Do you want me to stop?" Will asks.

"I'm on the phone," I say to him. Then, back to Operation Sigmund.

"It's really important? What I do?" I say. I pretend to find it superficial, but in fact it may be the most important question: How do you choose to spend the bulk of your time on earth?

"Our clients are serious about finding love. We work for commitment-minded individuals. Call us back when you're ready to commit to a profession—you'll be more equipped to commit to a love relationship."

I recognize that bitter tone. She's single and took this job not in hopes of matching soul mates, but in hopes of getting first dibs on all the men who call to get hooked up. I'm the competition. She wants to make sure I don't sign on the dotted line and steal her soul mate.

"Love relationship?" I say. Love relationship sounds too much like TV doctor lingo, and yet I start to think I could use one. Then I remember the details of the last serious relationship I had before meeting Sam. His name was Drew. Our relationship ended in a showdown with Drew shouting at me outside of a restaurant.

He was yelling about his unhappiness over how our relationship was ending. "I thought we'd be married," Drew yelled. He was so angry when he was saying it, even today it seems like a scary prospect that I narrowly escaped.

Then I snap out of it and remember I'm being turned down by a dating service . . . I haven't even been given the opportunity to be turned down by an actual individual. A small business is turning me down.

The rejection doesn't quell my urge to take a giant proactive step toward my future children. Unfortunately, the only semirelated event that doesn't require a long-term commitment that I stumble upon is a class at the Learning Annex. They are offering something called Flirting 101. It costs sixty-five dollars. It's too cheap to give me any confidence that it might actually work. The reality is, if it costs sixty-five dollars, I probably already know it. If it cost a thousand dollars and I can't afford it, then I would really need it.

But when I reflect back on the day, which I have ample time to do, it's not the phone call I'll be thinking about. Will's good at massaging. That was unexpected.

Credit for Participating

PERRY PULLS SOME GLASSES out of his cabinet. He inspects two of them. Then gets out a white cloth napkin and starts shining up the glasses. Not good enough. He pulls out two more. They meet his standards. He uncorks a bottle of wine. Pours. He's not talking.

"What's wrong?" I ask.

Perry shakes his head.

"Is tonight a bad night? I can leave you alone," I say.

"No, it's okay," Perry says. "In a funk."

"Oh. This might cheer you up. I'm kind of attracted to one of my coworkers," I say. "He can't be more than twenty-five. He looks like he's sixteen. I thought he might be an intern. . . . It's bad enough that I sleep at my mother's; now I'm attracted to a young man I'm sure spends the better part of his weekend skateboarding."

"Next you'll be wearing braces. Don't do it; they just aren't right on adults," Perry says. "But as far as the lad goes, screw around while you can, because who knows what will happen tomorrow?"

"That's just it—for the past few months I've been acting like there's no tomorrow. Quitting jobs. Not having the courage to try to work through things with Sam. So why am I thinking about this guy whose office is thirty feet from my desk? If he goes to the bathroom, he can't get back to his office without my unlocking the door for him," I say. "It gives new meaning to codependency."

"Yep, one day Danny fabulous is buying you a night-shirt that says 'He's My Bitch,' and the next day three blank checks are missing from the back of your checkbook," Perry says.

"You're dating again?" I ask.

"I thought it was a date; turns out I was just being

robbed," Perry says. "I get it that we all lie in the beginning of relationships. We don't feel safe. We want to put our best foot forward. But he stole checks from my checkbook while I was asleep! Who does that?"

I drink my wine.

"Say something," Perry says.

"I know you're going to be mad if I say what I'm thinking," I say.

"No, I'm not," Perry says.

Yes he is!

"Okay, are you taking a different medication?" I ask.

Perry tends to blame any poor behavior on his antidepressants or antianxiety medications.

He watches me for a while.

"I had a really shitty night, and I can't believe you'd ask me if it was because of new medication," Perry says.

"You're right," I say. "I'm sorry. It does sound like a bad night. But I really don't agree that we all lie when we're getting to know someone. That's your cynical point of view. It's not fact."

"You're kidding, right?" Perry says. "At least I'm talking about it. Your mother gets the big wake-up call. Your father reappears. The only thing in your life you seem certain about is that guy Sam. You never talk about any of it? That's lying. It's omitting the shit that matters to you."

Long pause. We both sip wine.

"Who said I was normal?" I ask. "By the way, you're an ass."

Perry gets up from the table and hugs me.

"Unfortunately, you're right," I say.

"Of course I am," Perry says.

"I need to know. Did you wear the nightshirt?" I ask.

"Yes, you know I love gifts."

T-shirt Fiesta

I FOLLOW PERRY into his store on St. Mark's Place. It was the first store he opened. He didn't plan to become the king of iron-on decals. It evolved. He opened his first store when he was at NYU film school. Then he dropped out after he opened his second store during his junior year. He didn't have time to file corporate taxes and attend classes. He has five stores in New York City.

"Are you allowed to drink wine and operate the heat press?" I ask.

"Drunk customers don't generally notice tipsy clerks," Perry says.

We enter the T-shirt Fiesta. A party indeed! There are piñatas hanging from the ceiling and confetti on the floor. He made prop half-emptied drinks and crumbled cocktail napkins placed strategically here and there. In the early days, he also sold frozen margaritas in Coca-Cola cups, to go, without a liquor license.

On the walls are colorful examples of things you might want to put on your very own T-shirt should you ever be drunk enough to buy a fifty-dollar T-shirt.

A pink T-shirt boasts the phrase: "Eat Shit. It's Free." For the expectant mom there is a cotton onesie in which to bundle her new baby: "When I cry, Mommy drinks!" And for the proud grandparents, a cute mini-T with a dual message: "Granny's a whore" (front of shirt), "Grandpa's a skank" (back of shirt).

"People actually spend money on these things?" I say.

"Yeah, isn't it depressing?" Perry says. "These letters are a buck a piece, and you wouldn't believe some of the long-ass messages people are willing to write."

"Like?" I say.

He motions toward another sample shirt on the wall: "I apologize in advance for anything I might do tonight!"

"Forty-five bucks just for letters and punctuation. That doesn't even include the shirt. And those are the jack-asses who want a discount. If I have to unpeel and line up forty-five letters, you're paying full price," Perry says.

"The way you've grown this business is amazing. You have to be proud of what you've accomplished," I say.

"Thanks, Grandma. It means a lot to me to make you proud," Perry says.

"You've always been so good about accepting compliments," I say. "You know, one of the biggest surprises about seeing my father after so many years was how much we look alike, and how comforting that is," I say.

"That's nice," Perry says.

It's more important than I would have guessed. I think

that comes from feeling so disconnected. Any connection becomes more significant than it should be. I don't look anything like my mother. People were always eyeing us as if we were the odd couple. I hated it.

"Loss is never one-sided," I say. "Maybe most of the pain that comes from loss is that people imagine it is one-sided."

As a child, I created a snapshot in my head. My father is carrying a medium-size suitcase and walking down the street. He is packed lightly. He is ready to start fresh in the world. He has no need to bring too much of his old life into his new life. There is no looking back for him. That mental image is a lifetime admission to anxietyville.

When my father left, it was a surprise. That ruined surprises for me. I needed things organized from that time on, like my mom does. I need a schedule, need to know what happens next. Spending time with him again doesn't erase any of that. But I do love the unexpected details I'm gleaning. I can't collect enough of them. They are tiny clues to knowing him. Precious tiny clues. He irons his own shirts "to make them last longer." He reads only the front page of a newspaper. No jump page for him. No sports section. No time? No desire? Who knows. Even he doesn't know. It's just what he's always done, so he continues to do it that way.

Honesty

IT'S NOT UNTIL LATER, after leaving Perry, when I'm walking uptown, that I rerun Perry's comments in my head.

"Don't we all lie in the beginning of a relationship?" Perry had said. What shocked me was how much I'd lied, as he said, by omission. Because of how much I haven't told anyone.

1. I've never had a mammogram, and I stopped doing self-exams after my mother was diagnosed, because I was afraid I'd find something I didn't want to find.
2. I'm pretty sure I'm in love with Sam, and I haven't told him. Okay, I'm doing it again. I'm soft-pedaling it. I'm not pretty sure. I'm sure. I'm in love with Sam.
3. Every day that I avoid the abovementioned, I become more and more like my mother.

I'm not sure which is scariest, 1, 2, or 3. . . .

Clean Bill of Health

SHE DOESN'T WANT to go anywhere special, Mom says. She just wants to enjoy lunch somewhere, knowing that the radiation treatments are completed. We choose an

Austrian place off of Fifth Avenue. There are a lot of German-speaking tourists eating spaetzle.

We make a toast with our glasses of ice water.

"Congratulations," I say.

"Thanks. It doesn't seem real," Mom says. "Does it?"

"To me it does," I say. "But I know what you mean; it may need to sink in."

I look up and see a familiar face. Mom's friend Phil comes toward us with his big happy face.

He takes a seat next to my mother. They hold hands. They exchange a stream of nonstop kisses on their cheeks.

"It's just so wonderful," Phil says.

"It really is," Mom says. "All those relaxation exercises paid off."

I look at the menu so I don't have to think about what that could be a euphemism for.

To Be Continued

IT'S FRIDAY. I get into the elevator with my father. He presses the button. He turns to me.

"Bowling ball, number two pencil, anemone, hot shoe, tension column, carboniferous reptile, and hydraulic brake hose," Jim says. "Your turn."

"Bowling ball, number two pencil, anemone, hot shoe, tension column, carboniferous reptile, hydraulic brake hose, and frangipani tree," I say, not looking at him.

"Bowling ball, number two pencil, anemone, hot shoe, tension column, carboniferous reptile, hydraulic brake hose, frangipani tree, and antibiotics," Dad says.

Where are those senior moments he's supposed to be experiencing?

Too Empathetic

I'M IN MOM'S KITCHEN trying to slice a pineapple. I feel like I'm shucking oysters.

"This is impossible," I say. "I don't think it's ripe."

"Marjorie had no problem cutting up my tropical fruits last week," Mom says. "If you don't know how, it's okay. I can call Marjorie."

"Okay, call her," I say.

"Well, I'm not going to bother her now; she's on bed rest," Mom says.

"They sell these things fully filleted now," I say.

"Still enjoying work?" Mom asks, changing the subject.

"Yes. The people are nice," I say. "The time goes quickly. I can't believe I've been there four weeks. I'm surprised by how much I like him."

"Like who?" Mom says.

"Dad," I say. It's the first time I've called him Dad.

"You're nothing like him," Mom says.

"I didn't say I was like him, I said I was surprised *that* I like him," I say.

"He can be very charming," Mom says.

Charming is code for unfaithful. My mother is still very much a lady. Ladies do not discuss men who stray.

"I wonder if it was difficult for him, just leaving home like that and never really knowing us afterward," I say. "It must have been."

"You're too empathetic, " Mom says. "You can always imagine the other side, and so you can't quite get mad at anyone, can you? I don't think that's healthy."

It's the truest thing she's ever said to me.

"We're spending too much time together, Mom; it's starting to drive me a little crazy," I say.

"Yes, I sensed that," Mom says. "But I so enjoy the company."

One Bad Apple

MY SANITY SAVIOR for the moment arrives in the form of a potential client. Or so I think. My guess is that he's in his fifties. He keeps calling saying he needs to talk to a lawyer "pronto." When I explain he needs an appointment, he hangs up. Then I imagine he walks around his hovel of an apartment wringing his hands, drinking beer, then dialing again. In order to get a different result, you need to have a different response. So I do. This time.

"Civil or criminal?" I ask.

"Criminal," he says.

"Violent or nonviolent," I ask.

"They say violent, but I was just tryin' to help," he says.

"Well, we have many qualified attorneys; unfortunately, they're all busy. So you can make an appointment and come in next week," I say.

"It can't wait," he says.

He also sounds like he can't pay.

"Can I just explain it to you?" he says.

"I've got a few minutes," I say.

"Long story short," he says. "I'm volunteering at this suicide hotline and this guy calls and he's miserable and he says he's going to kill himself. He starts telling me about his awful life—no job, no wife, house burnt down, car was stolen, twice. No auto insurance. He has Lyme disease. No health insurance. He's allergic to every food imaginable. He's manic-depressive. Nothing about his life is easy. So he calls three days in a row saying he's going to kill himself because he's so miserable. I try an' talk him out of it. Then the fourth day he calls, and I'm like, Look, buddy, meet me at Pier fifty-seven tonight at six P.M. I get there. I push 'im in. I jump in after 'im. I hold 'im under water for forty seconds. No dice. I'm tellin' ya, he had gills or something. I hold 'im under a minute. He's kickin' like a mother. Well, turns out the son of bitch *didn't* really want to die after all, and now he's pressing charges, sayin' I tried to kill 'im."

"You tried to drown him?" I say.

"Tried my best," he says.

"Was this protocol recommended in the volunteer handbook?" I ask.

"No, but at some point it's put up or shut up," he says.

"Acquiring that level of misguided conviction is almost artful," I say. "It's borderline impressive. Now, you'd been volunteering for the hotline how long?" I ask.

"A month," he says.

"This was your first attempted murder?" I ask.

"Are they gonna ask that?" he asks.

"Who?" I ask.

"The cops," he says.

"I don't know. I was just curious," I say. "Listen, you're not volunteering anymore, are you?"

" 'Course I am, I'm not letting one bad apple spoil it for the rest," he says.

"*You* are the bad apple," I say.

There is a pause. "That's tricky; are the cops going to say tricky things like that?" he asks.

"I don't know, I'm a receptionist. I'm not a cop," I say.

He hangs up.

Lunch Break

AT LUNCHTIME, I use my minutes wisely. I have forty of them. The elevator up and down eats up four minutes. Just thirty-six minutes left. I go to the bank. I buy a bottle of water. I have twenty-six minutes left. I've never been more aware of how much time matters.

I line up for a salad at a place that offers sixty salad toppings. I get overzealous, due to the mountain of choices. I get hard-boiled eggs, mushrooms, shredded cheese, chickpeas, avocado, tofu, green peas, and bacon all heaped onto lettuce then shaken together with their house dressing. It was fun making it. But once it's all combined, I have no desire to eat it. I pay for it and walk down Fifth Avenue.

Fifteen minutes to go. I sit on the steps of the New York Public Library and try to catch some spring sunshine. I open the salad and start to eat. I see a pea on my fork. The size of a pea . . . I think about cancer and feel nauseous. I put the salad back in the bag. So I watch people. There are people kissing. People talking to themselves. People spitting.

I see my father and a woman eating hot dogs next to the hot dog and gyro stand. They are fifteen yards away from me. When they are finished eating, my father squeezes the woman's shoulder. They hug. Then they walk in separate directions. He looks happy, but his steps seem heavy, in slow motion. He's getting older. The opportunity to know my father as a younger person is gone.

I stand up. Six minutes to get back to work. I think about my father hugging the woman just moments ago. He's making much better use of his lunchtime than I am. He gives me an idea.

Postcard

I BUY A POSTCARD and stamp in the library gift shop. I take a pen out of my purse and, in large type, I write:

Dear S.,

There is so much to say. Unfortunately, it won't all fit on this postcard.

E.

I surprise myself by mailing it.

Wacky Sock Day

TODAY IS WACKY Sock Day. I'm wearing a pair of rainbow-colored knee-highs. My father is wearing socks with crossword puzzles on them. This is depressing. It indicates he does pay *some* attention to detail . . . yet for two decades he managed not to remember he had a family.

"I look forward to this day all year long," says Wendy. "It lightens the mood and gives everyone a chance to express their creativity." Her socks feature different colored cats, all playing with balls of yarn.

"Since when is buying a pair of socks that aren't just black or blue considered to be the creative process?" I ask.

"Don't be a spoilsport!" Wendy says. "I look for fun socks every time I'm in a clothing store. It wasn't a coincidence that I found these. I hunted for these. I saved them for to-day."

"Maybe you all could sign up for a pottery class or something—so we can put an end to this collective hu-miliation. I'm no spoilsport; I wore the socks, didn't I?" I say. "People were hissing at me on Fifth Avenue when I was coming into the building. I don't want to start my day that way."

"Rookie mistake," says Wendy. "You put the socks on when you get to work. You don't wear them to work. Think of riding the subway and imagine the person most likely to get mugged—it would be the person with the cute socks, right? They make a person look so innocent. Like a victim. It's okay, you didn't know. Well, I'm off to organize the trash bags in the kitchen. Someone keeps mixing the six-gallon mini-bags in with the thirty-two-gallon kitchen-size bags."

Will steps off the elevator. There's something appeal-ing about his shaggy-dog, I-could-live-on-$12-a-week look. He's wearing navy socks with pinpoint white dots. Ah, wacky for him. He is a monochromatic sock guy. Navy. Black. Khaki. No stripes. No disruptive variations on the theme. I buzz him in, quickly, because if I leave him out by the elevators too long someone else might grab him before I decide if I want to or not.

"That's a great idea," I say, staring at his ankles.

"What?" Will says.

"Subjective wackiness," I say. I imagine us much later, in year two of our unlikely odd-couple marriage. I will learn that he has a sock "theory." He buys them in bulk, so when they get lost or mismatched, well, they don't. When you have ten pairs of the same socks, you don't spend much time sorting. The day he tells me this—confides really—I will start the "Will's Economy of Time File." Throughout the happy course of our marriage, I will add gems here and there. We will create oddball traditions of our own. And then it hits me: I am imagining a future. I never do that.

"Are you sticking around tonight?" Will asks.

"For what?" I say.

"No one told you? It happens only once every one hundred twelve years or something, when Pluto's moons are all in line. Wacky Sock Day coincides with Thirsty Thursday," Will says.

"Pluto has only one moon," I say. "What's Thirsty Thursday?"

"Beers in the conference room after hours," Will says. "Why do you know that Pluto has one moon?"

"I have a lot of time to read," I say. "Did you know that Mercury and Venus have no moons? Jupiter has sixty-two."

"A two-class solar system," Will says.

"Not really, Earth has one, and you don't see people losing any sleep over it," I say. "One seems like plenty. Maybe sixty-two are too many. Maybe a lot isn't a good thing in the case of moons. How special would a full moon be if you had a chance to see sixty-two of them?" *Stop talking! For the love of God, Emily, just stop talking!*

"You've given this some thought, haven't you?" Will says.

"I guess I have," I say.

I'm the one who will eventually get to leave. I need to remember that. But for now, the invitation is appealing. Something tells me my predecessor Esther never missed a Thirsty Thursday.

Toward the end of the day, there is a palpable energy in the air. A quiet thrill is waiting to be unleashed. It is five fifty-five . . . Wendy steps off the elevator. I buzz her in. She carefully maneuvers a pushcart. A chariot. She's the hero who gets to roll in all of that wonderful beer. No expense has been spared. Winter ales. Light beer. Japanese beer. Mexican beer. It's an eye-popping tower of chilled hops.

No great decorative preparations are made on Thirsty Thursday. All the money is in "product." This surprises me.

"No decorations?" I say to Wendy.

"Oh, good idea! You be in charge of those for next month," Wendy says.

"I'm not sure I'll be here next month," I say. "Besides, I thought it seemed like something you'd enjoy doing."

"I'm really more of an idea person," Wendy says.

"Okay," I say.

My father walks over and hands me a beer.

"It's a twist top," Dad says, sounding jubilant that someone thought to invent such a convenient way to get a bottle of beer opened.

"I see that," I say. "Thanks."

"I just knew you'd enjoy working here," Dad says. "It's a bevy of activity. All thanks to Wendy."

She smiles from across the room. Wendy is in love with my dad.

"How long has Wendy been working here?" I ask.

"I don't know," Dad says. "A few years. Quite a while, actually."

"A few? It's been fifteen years," I say. "She told me today."

"Has it really been that long?" Dad says.

"Time flies," I say.

"Yes, it does, doesn't it?" Dad says. He takes a sip of his beer.

Herman from billing wants to know how much people will pay him to drink six beers in under ten minutes. People start throwing money on the table. I think Herman might do this at home, for free, so I don't put any money on the table. It's a diversion. Herman is looking for free beer, fast. Not money. People are always more strategic than you expect them to be.

I sit down in a swivel chair. I peel the label off the

beer bottle. It's an undocumented symptom of obsessive-compulsive disorder. I think about crafting a letter to a psychological journal and letting them know about the label-peeling thing. I decide I'll write it first thing tomorrow. I'll put it on the firm's letterhead so it might be received with more excitement and regard.

"Is this seat taken?" Will asks.

"No," I say.

"A label peeler, huh?" Will asks.

I nod.

"In college that meant a girl was easy," Will says.

Mental note to self: Skip writing letter to psychological journal.

Just then another employee stands on the table and says she wants to know how much people will pay for Herman to drink two beers at once. Herman takes his newly earned cash, sticks it in his pocket, and climbs on to the table.

"Two beers at once? I'll do it for free," Herman says.

Of course he will! These people have it right, I suppose. They are at least inventing ways to collide into each other, get closer.

Labor

GROWING UP, OUR KITCHEN had ecru-colored walls, eggshell finish, with some mica powder rubbed into it. It looked like fairy dust. We weren't allowed to touch the walls.

Marjorie used to walk into our kitchen and touch the walls, while asking my mother a seemingly innocent question. It drove my mother crazy. That's the difference between Marjorie and me. She'd touch the walls to make my mother angry. I went out of my way to do things perfectly, because my mother was already angry with me for being too much like my father.

"Please don't do that, Marjorie!" Mom would say.

"Sorry," Marjorie would say, smiling. She'd touch the wall again.

"Damnit, Marjorie!" my mother would say. "Stop touching the walls with those filthy hands!"

It's three-thirty in the morning. My mother knocks on my door. She hands me the phone. When she calls in the middle of the night—in labor—Marjorie is still touching the walls. At least that's how my mother sees it.

"This has got to stop. Please tell your sister not to call after nine P.M.," Mom says.

"Why don't you tell her!" I ask.

"You better get dressed. She's in labor," Mom says.

"Maybe that's why she's calling in the middle of the night, Mom! Marjorie?" I say, taking the phone from Mom's outstretched hand. "What do you want me to do?"

"Malcolm's in the air. Literally. He's coming home from London. I'll take a cab to Mom's place; I'll be there in a few minutes. Can you wait out front and come with me? Malcom's—ohhhhh . . ."

On *The Passionate & the Youthful,* they deliver babies

everywhere except in a delivery room. So I know babies can be born in cabs, in elevators, in locker rooms, in restaurants, and at major sporting events. In each case, someone "coaches" the mother-to-be. Coaching mainly involves reminding the person to breathe. Then offering lots of congratulations when the mother-to-be does breathe.

"Marjorie, you can do this. Breathe," I say.

I hear her breathing on the other end. I immediately like coaching and find it very rewarding, even though you say very obvious things that the other person would be doing anyway. Somehow, I still feel like I'm doing a good job and that I am, at the moment, irreplaceable. I feel needed. I like that.

"You're doing great," I say. "I'll be downstairs in five minutes; remember your suitcase. I know you bought new luggage for this, so be sure to bring it with you!"

"Ohhh . . ."

"Bring a camera, too," I say.

"Oh, right, I have to find the camera," Marjorie says. "See you in a few minutes."

I brush my teeth and throw on jeans and a sweater. I grab my purse.

"Take a book," Mom yells from her bedroom. "It's a lot of hurry up and wait at that hospital."

"Thanks," I say. "Do you want to come along?"

"No, but if you get tired, I can take over," Mom says. "Call me."

Baby

LITTLE MALCOLM HAS the most perfect little round head and big blue eyes. The tiniest feet and fingers. They seem too tiny to function. His lips and skin are red, and his hair is jet black. He looks like a skinny wet kitten. I can't help but stare in amazement at the only seven pounds that could ever truly change Marjorie's world.

They weigh him and measure him, and roll his feet on an ink pad. What a clumsy introduction to the world. I get to hold him while Marjorie is being taken care of. He looks at me. He's studying me. Staring at my enlarged pores. I turn my head. He keeps looking, the unrelenting observer.

I whisper in his ear, confiding: "I've tried facials, I've tried minimizers. Nothing works!" He smiles. He knows stuff. He burps, and in that burp, I'm convinced, was a message: Try alpha hydroxy.

"He's so sweet. I'll baby-sit sometime if you're in a pinch," I say.

"Okay," Marjorie says. Then, to the doctor, "It feels like World War II down there . . . is that the way it's supposed to feel?"

"Well, yes, but you shouldn't be feeling it," the doctor says. She opens the floodgates on Marjorie's IV. Less than a minute later Marjorie gives a thumbs-up sign, and falls asleep.

Big Malcolm arrives, jet-lagged, just in time to accompany Little Malcolm to his first bath. Once the baby has been whisked away, Marjorie is moved to a new room.

She insists on changing into some expensive Egyptian cotton pajamas. So Joanie! I brush her hair.

"I want to kiss that epidural guy," Marjorie says.

"You always did go for Mr. Popular," I say.

"Only because I'm not thoughtful enough to find a diamond in the rough," Marjorie says. "What can I say? I'm not a worker bee."

"You just spent fifteen hours in labor," I say. "And you have the energy to imagine hypothetically kissing the anesthesiologist. You work much harder than you give yourself credit for."

"Then why can't I be bothered to pick out my own clothing?" Marjorie asks.

"I don't know. Because stores are too big now. It takes forever to shop," I say. "Tell me you're not hiring a personal shopper for the baby's clothing, though."

"No," Marjorie says. "I'll enjoy doing that."

I am no longer needed here. But being needed felt great while it lasted.

Light on Affection

I TAKE INVENTORY of my current situation and place in the world. I have a mind-numbing job—luckily temporary. I have a law degree, coupled with a fading interest in the law. My mother is doing pretty well. I can move back into my own home. . . . No word from Sam. No acknowledgment of the postcard I sent him. Will walks by.

He says what he always says.

"Emily, want some coffee?"

"No, but thanks for asking," I say.

Which is what I always say. But this time, I want a different outcome, some hope. "But I'd love a Perrier," I say.

I believe this is just the sort of optimistic yes-you-can-do-something-for-me response Will has been waiting for. He brings me the Perrier.

"Thanks," I say.

"Sure," Will says. "Hey, I want to show you something in my office."

His shirtless torso? His chiseled scales-of-justice-lifting biceps? No, instead we look at some photos he's taken. Exhibit A: his sensitive side.

We sit on his couch. Our knees touch. We both react as if we've just touched a hot teakettle with bare flesh—and move away from each other in a panic. He opens an art portfolio. They are nice lawyer-turned-weekend-photographer-type photos. He developed them himself. There are shots taken in Central Park. Street musicians. Trees. The Great Lawn. Several photos fall out of a pocket of the book. I pick them up, and he reaches over to take them from me.

"Oh, come on, let me see them," I say. "I'm sure this is what you really wanted to show me anyway."

There are six photographs of a brown-haired woman with large eyes and a healthy amount of cleavage. In one shot she's lying in bed, covered by a sheet but not wearing clothing.

"Your sister?" I ask.

"Funny woman!" Will says. "Former girlfriend."

"She's very pretty," I say.

"It's all makeup and trick photography. She's hideous in real life," Will says.

"When did she dump you?" I ask.

"A few weeks ago," Will says.

When we finish looking at the photos, he closes the black folder and ties the string that closes it.

There is a knock at the door. It opens, and Wendy is standing there with a manila envelope and a staff list. Still seated on the couch, Will's knees fall into mine again. I don't move this time. Neither does he. Our knees rest against each other, under his portfolio.

"I knew there was something going on in here. Don't worry, I'll never tell," Wendy cackles. "I'm collecting money for cake and Chinese food. I need seven dollars from each of you."

"Whose birthday is it?" I ask. "Must be someone important if you're springing for Chinese food."

"Mine," Wendy says.

"Couldn't someone else plan your party?" I ask. "I can collect money if you want."

"Control freaks don't let other people plan their parties," Wendy says. "That's not the way it works."

I give Wendy a ten-dollar bill and tell her to keep the change. Will walks over to his desk. The top left drawer is filled with coins.

"Did you ever figure out how many scoops equal five dollars?" Will asks.

"You were going to do that calculation," Wendy says.

"Let's call it two," Will says.

"I told you I'm not taking coins anymore," Wendy says.

"Suit yourself," Will says, closing the drawer.

Wendy leaves.

"I should go back to my desk," I say. "Thanks for showing me the photographs of the park and the nearly nude shots of your ex-girlfriend."

"Can we have—do you want to go out sometime?" Will says.

"Sure," I say. "Sometime." Sometime? Vague and open-ended—just the way I like it.

"Tomorrow night?" Will asks. He can't be more than twenty-five, and he's acting even younger.

"Tomorrow?" I say. It's a surprise. I don't like surprises.

But I have no readily available excuse, and I have nowhere else to go. "Sure."

I walk down the hall toward the bathroom, to see what I look like. What did I look like when Will was just looking at me?

I pass the kitchen. I watch from the doorway as my father fixes his stare on the microwave oven. Wendy scolds him about spoiling his lunch. Why eat popcorn when Chinese is on the way? He laughs.

An office wife is really the answer. She is the perfect mate for him. She can look up to him. He's a good boss. He's even a thoughtful boss. He can empathize with his bored and unhappy employees because he's bored and unhappy on the job, too. A person living with him might never see how empathetic he can be. He's a better person at work than he is at home. He's figured this out. That's what impresses me most. He's figured it out.

Father's Keeper

I LOOK NICE TODAY. My father wonders why, but he can't bring himself to ask. He either doesn't want to know about any potential sex life I might have, or he thinks saying I look nice will point out that most of the time I'm lucky if my shoes match.

He likes it that we share a cab to work. He and his girl going off to fight crime in the big city. We can pretend he wasn't AWOL for the last twenty years. The cab ride is one of the few uncomplicated things we share. So we both try to enjoy it. This is the level to which things have come. We don't want to talk about the past, or my mother, or my career, or his depression. Instead, let's become absorbed in this fabulous cab ride. You don't realize how much of the world is cordoned off by glass until you are seeking protection. Running for cover. There is a thick sheet of plastic separating us from the driver, and then there is all of the invisible stuff that separates my father and me. I like the straightforwardness of the plastic divider. This is my side, that's yours. No ambiguity. No guessing.

"They call that a safety precaution?" I say mockingly to Dad, motioning toward the divider.

"Doesn't hold a candle to the Plexiglas shield you enjoy each and every day," Dad says. "Do you want to have dinner tonight? Your mother could join us."

"Thanks. I wish I could, but I have plans tonight," I say. And if I didn't, I might just pretend I did to avoid such a weird interaction.

"What kind of plans?" Dad says, in a tone that could possibly be indicating he's up for whatever kind of sassy arrangements are on deck.

"Dinner plans," I say.

"Do I know him?" Dad asks.

"Yeah, he works four offices down the hall from you," I say. "You hired him."

"Bob? He's a married man. I didn't know he was having trouble at home. I don't think that's the sort of thing a bright young woman should be getting involved with," he says, as if he were talking about someone other than me. "I always thought he was a stand-up guy. A model of good behavior."

I want to strangle him. Now. In public.

"Bob is *three* offices down," I say. "You think I'd date a Mormon with four kids? Thanks."

"Oh. Will. He's a smart one," Dad says. "Young, though."

Wearer of conservative shirts. Keeps diplomas hung in corner, as if embarrassed by an abundance of education. Lips that appear to be perfect for kissing. I could go on, but my father is staring.

"Yeah," I say. "He's smart."

"Does he still have his friend?" Jim asks. "The girl?"

"His girlfriend?" I ask.

"Yes. I thought he was involved with someone," Jim says.

Will's apparently shown *everyone* the half-naked photos of his girlfriend.

"I think it ended," I say. At least that's the story he's telling.

Chiclets

WILL IS AT the newsstand in the lobby. He's deciding whether to buy Chiclets or Tic-Tacs. This seems sweet to me. That he's taking this meaningless choice seriously. What will he treat his mouth to today? His tongue has been so very good to him. And his teeth and gums, too. They all deserve a pick-me-up . . . will he favor them with a delicious smorgasbord? Gum and mints? Or perhaps something to harass his teeth—Jujyfruits?

"Emily, I need to ask you something," Will says.

"Chiclets," I say. I hope he picks the fruity kind. Peppermint and spearmint just seem too noncelebratory. The workhorses of the breath-freshener family.

"Do you think any kissing will occur tonight?" Will asks.

I stare at him for a while. "Tonight?" I ask.

"Between you and me," Will says. "On our date."

"Oh," I say. Good lord, what have I agreed to? "I don't know," I say. But that question alone makes me seriously doubt it.

"You don't *know*? Sounds like a yes to me! Do you have a strong preference between wintergreen and peppermint?" Will asks.

"Strong preference? No," I say.

I stare at him. I stare at him because when our knees touched yesterday I did feel something. It was exciting.

Before I meet Will for dinner, I stop at a pay phone. I call Sam. If he answers, it means I will cancel dinner plans with Will. But Sam doesn't answer. Maybe he's in the shower. I wait ten minutes. I call again. Still no answer. I leave a message.

"Hi. Emily here. I was calling to say . . . 'Hi, Emily here,'" I say. "Maybe I'll call again in a few minutes."

I hang up the phone. I'm still doing it. I'm calling Sam to keep me away from Will, and I'm here to meet Will in hopes that it will keep me away from Sam. One foot out of two different doors.

Red Formica Table

WE MEET IN the West Village at Two Boots for pizza. He kisses my cheek as he opens the door to the restaurant for me. I'm not sure if he's being sincere, or mocking this "date."

Will is wearing jeans and a T-shirt and running shoes. There is a rubber band around his calf to hold his pants out of the way of his bicycle chain.

My clothing is all wrong for this part of town. I'd have to buy a new wardrobe if things ever developed between us.

We take a seat at a red Formica table.

"Beer?" Will asks.

"Sure," I say.

"I hope you'll trust me to order," Will says.

"It's pizza," I say.

"Which is why I feel supremely confident," Will says.

The waitress comes over to the table. Will orders.

"Two light beers. Two salads. Dressing on the side for the lady. That okay with you? I know the ladies prefer the dressing on the side," Will says.

"Have a lot of experience with the ladies, do ya?" I say.

"And one Hawaiian pizza," Will says.

The waitress scribbles on her pad and disappears. I look around the place. A couple in their thirties is eating pizza with their twin boys. The rest of the tables are filled with teenagers.

"Should we talk shop?" Will asks.

"Okay," I say.

"Who spends more time on the phone? Me or Wendy?" Will asks.

"Too close to call," I say. "You're both kind of chatty."

There is an awkward pause. Will contemplates the pepper shaker.

"Are you starting to think we ruined the romance by moving this outside of the office?" Will asks. "I was really enjoying all of that sexual tension at work."

"Have you talked to your girlfriend recently?" I ask.

"She won't call me back," Will says.

"Oh," I say. "What did you do?"

"Told her I loved her," Will says. "What's your story?"

"No story," I say. "Nothing I'm telling you anyway."

For a moment I feel tempted to excuse myself from the table and go to the nearest pay phone and call Sam again to tell him about the date I'm on. About the rubber band on Will's pant leg. Maybe he'd get in a cab and rescue me from this funny earnest person who seemed more like a younger brother than someone to kiss.

"So, do you love her?" I ask.

"I don't know. I thought I did," Will says. "But it's not easy to love someone who won't return your phone calls."

"Right," I say.

Will comes around to my side of the table and sits next to me on the Formica bench. He puts his hand under my chin. He kisses me. I kiss him back.

"Get a room!" one of the teenagers yells.

Bicycle Built for Two

AFTER TWO BOOTS, we ride Will's bike to Grange Hall for another glass of wine.

"I think it's time for me to go home now," I say. "Thanks, Will, it was a fun night."

"Yeah?" Will says.

"Yeah," I say.

"Can I give you a ride to Hudson? You can catch a cab going uptown," Will says.

I climb back onto the front handlebars, and lift my feet up, and balance myself.

Romance at the workplace is not a good idea. Extremely light emphasis on the word "romance," please. Will is not ready for marriage or love or even a bicycle built for two. I could stagnate here, I suppose. Choosing Will is an emotional cop out. But at some point I must learn to finish and not just start.

When I get home, I play my messages. There's only one.

"Hi, Em. I'll try you again, even if you call only when you can't really talk," Sam says.

A Pet

I RETURN FROM lunch on Monday. On my desk is a mystery. A small fishbowl. Inside is a goldfish, swimming in circles. Exploring. All alone and going nowhere, like someone else I know.

I dial Will's extension.

"Hello?" Will says.

"Did you buy the goldfish?" I ask.

"No," Will says. "I'm with a client. Wait, who's buying you goldfish? Man, that's really good. Flowers are nice, but a goldfish is so much better."

"Maybe it's not for me," I say.

Or maybe someone grew bored with it and dropped it off here. The way people drop unwanted cats off at farms?

Jim walks by.

"Do you like him?" Jim asks.

"You bought the goldfish?" I say.

"Yes," Jim says. "I thought you could use some company out here."

Is this his polite way of saying my wiretapping has got to stop?

"Thanks!" I say. "That's very sweet."

My reaction to the fish surprises me. I'm elated to have this bowl sitting on my desk. I must be lonelier than I thought.

"What are you going to call him?" Jim asks.

"I don't know," I say.

"He's a happy guy," Jim says.

"How can you tell?" I ask.

"Can't you tell? I can just tell," Jim says.

He did seem to be happily swimming, but what are his options?

I move him to the left of my desk so his bowl is not directly below the air-conditioning vent. I sit back in my chair and watch Happy.

EVERY DAY AT about two, the air conditioner gets too cold, so I open the window and hear the sounds of traffic below on Sixth Avenue. A man on the street is holding a public sermon warning, announcing that Jesus is coming. I imagine the cold air spiraling out of the window, dancing down the building, and caressing his cheek, like the hand of God. A reward for believing.

Like a Diamond in the Sky

I'M SITTING AT my desk when the phone rings. My line. My direct line never rings. Marjorie doesn't even say hello. She starts a tirade.

"Guess what the in-laws got him?" Marjorie says.

"Got who?" I ask.

"Baby Malcolm," Marjorie says. "As a gift for being born."

"Carton of Marlboro Lights?" I ask.

"*That* would have been *useful*." Marjorie sighs.

"Sterling silver something?" I ask.

"Too girlie," Marjorie says.

"Gift certificate to a steakhouse?" I say.

"Nope. They named a star after him . . . and sent us the official certificate of authenticity. It even came with a map," Marjorie says.

"That's kind of sweet," I say. "He can't even sit up yet, and he's already got his own star? That kid's life is going to be great!"

"Would a cute outfit have been too much to ask for? We don't have two nickels to rub together, and they're buying real estate in outer space?" Marjorie says.

"It would be difficult to be your mother-in-law," I say.

"Why?" Marjorie says.

"Because sometimes it's difficult being your sister,"

I say. "It's not their fault you guys spend every cent you have. How much money have you spent on purses alone this year? More than most people spend on a car! You have a personal shopper for fuck's sake! When you're too busy to do it yourself, she's out there spending money *for* you. It's insane. You don't get to complain about not having money when you blow through it the way you do."

"Remind me not to call you when I need a sympathetic ear. And it's not always easy being your sister, either. All this time you're spending with Mom and Dad can't be healthy. You're neurotic because you spent too much time with Mom after they divorced. Now you're just compounding your problems by working for Dad. . . . It's not normal," Marjorie says.

"Aren't you even curious what he's like? Why their marriage fell apart?" I ask.

"Not really. I don't live in the olden days," Marjorie says. "If you have children, you'll discover that there's a whole lot less time to worry about yourself and your parents. It's a happy relief to know the world doesn't revolve around Joanie and Jim. Anyway, I didn't call you to start a fight."

"I know. Just remember, it's nice that Malcolm has grandparents who are thinking about him. He's a really sweet baby, isn't he?" I say.

"Yes, and I already miss being pregnant," Marjorie says.

"It must be a very hopeful time," I say.

"Well, that and I had the metabolism of a teenager. I used to be able to eat a baguette and a wheel of Brie for lunch," Marjorie says.

Pimp My Bowl

ON THE WAY to meet my father to share a cab to work, I pass Petland Discounts. It must be where Dad bought Happy. I walk inside. It smells of dog. Happy traded up in a big way. He's the office darling.

I walk over to the fish equipment aisle. I select a net. Some water purifier. I'm about to go and pay when I see something Happy *has* to have. A treasure chest. The lid is propped open and a bounty of coins and jewels spill out. I buy some hot pink gravel and a floating thermometer and some live plants. Nothing's too good for Happy.

I see a miniature scuba guy. It offends me. I instantly recognize it as something that would scare Happy—being trapped in a bowl with a small man dressed in latex.

An hour later, Happy's home is transformed. It's so nice I wouldn't mind living in there.

I open the top drawer of my desk. I pull out a card. Mom's oncologist Dr. Kealy gave me the name of his favorite mammogram guy. They never miss anything, he said. If I have time to decorate a fishbowl, I probably have time to get a mammogram. Besides, Happy needs me.

Colic

WHENEVER I CALL Marjorie, it's a bad time. Big Malcolm is never home, and her baby nurse du jour has just quit, just stolen, or just broken something irreplaceable and needs to be fired.

"I'm a terrible mother," Marjorie says with a certain amount of pride and resignation. "At least I can admit it!"

"Do you need some help?" I ask.

"Yes. I need help, then I need cameras to watch the help. Then I need help firing the help. The first baby nurse took my engagement ring," Marjorie says.

"That's horrible. Where was the ring?" I ask.

"Hidden. I wasn't wearing it when I was pregnant because my hands were so swollen. So before I went to the hospital I put it inside of a sock, with some cash, and then put that inside of a rain boot in my closet. The money is gone, and so is the ring," Marjorie says. "She was here a few days before Malcolm was born to get things organized. She must have ripped the place apart as soon as I went into labor."

"What did the agency say?" I ask.

"Said I shouldn't have left any valuables around the house," Marjorie says.

"That's helpful," I say. "Why don't I come over?"

Little Malcolm is crying in the background throughout the conversation.

"You really don't want to. All this baby does is cry," Marjorie says. "No wonder Big Malcolm never comes home. I wish I didn't have to come home. I'm starving, and I can't seem to find time to order food."

"Just let me pick something up and come over; I promise I won't stay long," I say.

"Arrive at your own peril," Marjorie says. "Honestly, it's not pretty."

I borrow a six-pack of Yuengling from the conference room and call in an order to William Poll. I take a cab over to Lexington Avenue to pick up my little handmade crustless sandwiches on my way to Marjorie's.

When she opens the door, Malcolm is screaming. There are three strollers in the entryway. A swing. A bassinet. Tons of baby gear everywhere.

"I'm really sorry; I thought you were exaggerating," I say. "He really doesn't stop crying, does he?"

"No. Well, yes, occasionally. But the two baby nurses who didn't commit larceny said they'd never seen colic like this. Then they quit," Marjorie says.

"I can watch him for a while; do you want to take a shower?" I ask.

"That bad?" Marjorie says.

"No. I just thought you could use a break," I say. "It must be so hard to leave him," I say.

"Not really. I take out the garbage just to get some 'me' time," Marjorie says. "I never feel guilty. I envy these mothers who feel this sense of guilt."

Marjorie says "these" as if referring to two or three mothers, or characters from fiction, but not real life.

"As soon as I find a baby nurse who won't quit, I'm going to a spa in Napa for five days. Alone," Marjorie says.

I just assumed every mother knows how to take care of her own child better than any stranger ever could. And within seconds, I realize how absurd that thought is.

"I'd kind of like to hold him," I say.

"He's yours, take him," Marjorie says.

I rock him. I dance with him. I stand still with him. I try a pacifier. I try a bottle. I try music. I change his diaper. Still, he screams. I remember reading somewhere that babies like the sound of a vacuum cleaner because it replicates the noise they hear while in the uterus. Imagine sleeping next to a vacuum cleaner for forty weeks?

I buckle Malcolm into his swing. I turn it on. He screams. I start looking in closets for the vacuum cleaner. I find one cabinet that is devoted to Tupperware. The real stuff, not the cheapo knock-off Tupperware. No lid is attached to its bowl. Things are tossed about willy-nilly, which must serve as a huge deterrent from ever even opening that cabinet and enjoying such wonderfully overpriced containers. I can't leave the kitchen without first organizing that cabinet. Who wants a plastic waterfall spilling out onto her kitchen floor? It's not lost on me that I'm morphing into my mother. I can't control it. The scary thing is I don't even *want* to control it! I enjoy organizing. I see what the payoff is! Serenity! I complete the task and then remember I was looking for a vacuum. The best I can find is a Dust Buster. I race back to the living room.

Marjorie is standing in the doorway with a towel on her head. She's wearing a robe.

"What happened?" Marjorie says.

"Nothing. I heard that vacuum cleaners work," I say. "Is this all you have? A Dust Buster?"

"I don't know. Cleaning is not my department. How'd you get him to sleep?" Marjorie says. "He's cried every time we've put him in that swing."

"He screamed when I put him in it, too. I just needed a safe place to put him while I looked for the vacuum," I say.

He's sound asleep. I didn't even have a chance to turn on the Dust Buster.

"Maybe he's exhausted from the crying," I say. "What did the doctor say?"

"He said, 'Some babies just cry a lot and yours is one of them.'"

"Find a new doctor," I say.

What really shocks me is that people are *still* having babies. It just seems so strangely optimistic.

I unwrap the sandwiches and put them on plates. I make a salad. I open two beers. We sit on the couch, instead of at the table. Mainly because the table has become a diaper-changing station, where piles of unfolded laundry form soft sculptures.

"I'm not sold on his name. Little Malcolm. Maybe he

isn't, either. Maybe that's the problem. Maybe it's all a protest over his name." Marjorie turns to look at him, as if he were a car, or a pair of shoes she was contemplating returning.

"It's a *little* late for that, isn't it?" I say.

"I was just being lazy when I named him," Marjorie says.

"Oh, don't beat yourself up over it. You only had *nine* months to think of a name, which he'll only have *forever!*" I say.

"I thought it might charm Big Malcolm. You know, he wasn't exactly fired up for a baby, so I thought naming him Little Malcolm might help," Marjorie says.

"First off, I hope that 'big' was added only after the baby was born," I say. "Are you afraid that Little Mal will feel too much pressure to live up to the name?"

"You're forgetting who the original is," Marjorie says. "If he can drink a few scotches and still toss his underpants in the general direction of the hamper, he'll outshine his namesake."

It's eight-thirty. She looks tired.

"It's time for me to go," I say.

"Okay," says Marjorie.

"Call me if you need anything," I say.

"Okay, thanks for everything, especially the beer. And for telling me to take a shower," Marjorie says. "How's Mom?"

"Good," I say.

"Is it weird having Dad around?" Marjorie asks.

"Not as weird as I would have guessed," I say.

"Why do you stay involved with these people?" Marjorie asks.

It's as if I'm only supposed to ever have one parent. So the moment my mother becomes ill, my father grows remorseful for a lifetime of foolishness, and he tries to make up for two and a half decades of absent parenting. And I'm more than happy to let him try.

Slob Baby

UNTIL MY MOTHER got cancer, I didn't know a lot about my father. I certainly had no idea what a gigantic weenie he was. He can be truly infantile.

We are in a cab headed to work.

"Driver, stop!" Dad says.

"What is it?" I ask.

"The plants. We need to go back," Dad says. "I water the plants on Wednesday. I forgot. Wednesday can hardly continue without the plants being watered."

It's no joke. To his thinking, if the plants didn't get watered, Wednesday would have to be on hold. I get it. I had to organize Marjorie's Tupperware before I could leave the kitchen—but I thought I'd gotten that trait from my mom. Why couldn't I have inherited a love of opera?

Or something else that at least passes as a respectable hobby.

I look around his place while he takes the world's tiniest watering can and fills it. He waters one plant, and then needs to go back to the kitchen for a refill.

"If you got a larger watering can, you could do this in a fraction of the time," I say.

"I'm in no rush," Dad says. "Besides, this watering can is perfectly fine. There is nothing wrong with this watering can."

"Except that it's too small for the job," I say. "Maybe you had fewer plants when you bought it."

"It's the perfect watering can," Dad says.

I look in his bedroom. There is a wet towel on his bed. In his bathroom, there is a wet towel on the floor. I pick them up and hang them over his shower door.

He continues watering plants. His zipper is unzipped. In the kitchen there is an empty box of Popsicles in the trash can.

"What did you eat for breakfast?" I ask.

"Popsicles," Dad says.

"How many?" I ask.

"I don't know, four or five, why?" Dad says.

"Your tongue is blue. I noticed it in the cab. But it's blue every day. I always thought it was your mouthwash. Do you eat Popsicles for breakfast every day?" I ask.

"I'm a bachelor," Dad says.

"Is that a yes or a no?" I ask.

"What if I do?" Dad says.

"Just a question, really," I say. "Do whatever you want. But at least zip your fly."

He's the worst kind of slob baby I've ever seen.

I'm not sure what I expected. Having never lived with a man, and not having a father for most of my life, men are a bit of a mystery to me. He's a bachelor? I admire him for that—for confusing being alone with being a bachelor. In my opinion, if you're playing tricks on yourself, this is one worth playing. It's for the greater good.

I look into the kitchen. He's standing there in front of an open cabinet. There are a gaggle of pill bottles in front of him. He uses one hand to feed pills into his mouth, and the other to swill water. He alternates this motion at record speed. He fires pill after pill into his mouth.

We didn't come back to his place because he forgot to water plants. That part of this equation is reassuring. But it's hard not to be unsettled after seeing his colorful eye-popping collection of tablets, pills, and capsules.

Raw Meat

WE MEET AT BERGDORF's for deviled eggs and iced tea.

"I feel like a complete ass; I told my therapist I had a dream we had sex," I say. "Do you think I should have told him that?"

"Hell no, that's like throwing raw meat to a wild animal," Marjorie says. She thinks about it for a minute or two. "Were you telling the truth? Did you really have a dream about jumping him? Or were you flattering him so he'd refill your Xanax?"

"Right. I made it up, like I do with all the stuff I tell my therapist," I say.

"I'm still drunk from last night," Marjorie says. She can't stop laughing. "What does he look like? Is he cute?" More laughing. "Should I be seeing him, too? I got high last night; I still feel like I'm high."

"You still get high?" I ask.

For a time, her single greatest skill was being able to convert any household item into a marijuana pipe. A carrot, a soda can, a cardboard paper towel roll . . . It was like watching a true origami artist having a fit of genius. She was fast, creative, and the pipe always worked.

Once, when we were both on summer break from college, we went to East Hampton for a weekend. She read a self-improvement book from cover to cover while I drove. Later, I opened the book and saw that the only heavily underlined chapter was the one called "How to Come Across 100 Percent Authentic to Everyone You Meet."

Marjorie takes out a pack of Marlboro Lights and some matches. She lights a cigarette. She decided long ago to ignore the whole ban on public smoking thing.

"I thought you quit when you got pregnant," I say.

"I did," Marjorie says, still puffing. "But I'm not pregnant anymore. You're going to be proud of me. I fired

Nevin and Dory. No life coach, no food coach. *And* I cut the nanny back to part-time. I'm saving a lot of money, and I have no time to shop. It's working out okay so far."

The waiter taps Marjorie on the shoulder. He's going to tell her to put her cigarette out. It's going to get nasty. He's going to have to pry the carcinogen from her hand.

"We have a seat in the kitchen for you if you'd like to finish your cigarette there," the waiter says.

The world bends in her direction. Every day, it bends and twists to accommodate her. The topography molds, like wet clay, to hug her.

"Okay," Marjorie says. "Be right back."

I sit at the table finishing my iced tea. There are deviled egg carcasses still on the plate. I'm staring until the distance comes into focus. I see Sam, having lunch with a woman. Adults. They are having lunch and a glass of wine. I pretend I don't see him. I reorganize things in my wallet. I resist the urge to look his way again. But I can feel the pull of him. Eventually, I turn to steal another look, and he's gone.

Unanswered Letters

I LIE ON THE COUCH at home with a legal pad. I draw around the edges of the paper, too afraid to commit word to paper. I can't shake the image of Sam on the opposite side of the restaurant. Sam is as close to me and as far from me as my father used to be. I thought it had to be that way. It never occurred to me before that you could learn to move closer, even this late in life. I thought mothers were the ones who were responsible for teaching us how to love.

Dear Sam,

There is some freedom in writing a letter you know no one will answer. Some torture and regret, too, of course.

Just as I think I'm pushing myself (theoretically) forward, I catch a glimpse of you out in the real world. In other words, I saw you today at Bergdorf's having lunch. I pretended I didn't see you for about two minutes. I busied myself by tossing out old receipts and such from my wallet. When I turned around again you were gone.

My mother is recovering. I'm getting to know my father. There are days I feel lucky to be learning things about relationships that I should have learned when I was younger. And then there are mornings I wake up and get dressed and for several seconds I think I'm headed to my old job, and will be seeing you. When reality hits it always hurts.

You looked good and it was nice to see you. The wallet is organized now. Next time I'll say hello.

xo, Emily

Café Habana

I'M IN MY CHAIR at work, enjoying my lumbar support. It's a towel that I've rolled into a makeshift back-relief apparatus. Necessity is not the mother of invention. Boredom is.

I call my mom.

"I'm in for the night," she says.

"You sound exhausted. Are you okay?" I ask. It's only six o'clock.

"Just relaxing," Mom says.

"Okay, do you want me to bring dinner over to you?" I ask.

Her response is short and sweet, and in a whisper: "Honey, I'm not alone. Can I call you tomorrow?"

I try to stop myself, but an image of her tangled up on the davenport with Phil springs to mind.

"Good for you, Mom," I say. "Call you tomorrow."

"Okay, but not too early," Mom says.

Oh! I didn't need that much information. Will walks by the reception area.

"How are things?" Will says.

"Better than I thought," I say.

"Glad to hear it," Will says. "Your mom doing okay?"

"I think she has a date tonight," I say.

"Not a bad idea. How about Café Habana?" Will says.

"Oh," I say, thinking it might be nice to get away from work, home, and transient thoughts about Sam. "Sure. There's always room for Cuban corn."

Things start out nicely enough. The corn *is* good. But the tide shifts when Will's one or two beers turn into nine! That's 120 ounces of liquid! How is the human body supposed to cope?

The evening ends with my lifting Will's youthful head up from the table and asking him if he knows his own address. I put his bike into the trunk of a cab, and walk him up three flights of stairs to his apartment.

At least I no longer have to wrestle with the question of whether I'm judging him unfairly due to his youth.

Cold Drink

WE'RE BY THE WATERCOOLER. His eyes are bloodshot.

"What did you think about last night?" Will says.

"So you remembered we went out last night?" I ask. "What did *you* think about last night?"

"What I remember of it was stellar!" Will says. "Sorry for getting . . . drunk."

"It's okay," I say.

"Shall we try to recapture our magic tomorrow night?" Will asks.

"Another time, maybe," I say.

"Another time—maybe never, right?" Will says. "We're not going to kiss anymore, are we?"

"No," I say.

"Yeah, well, some guy, somewhere, just caught the break of a lifetime," Will says.

"Do you happen to know where he is? 'Cause he's not returning my calls and it's making me a little nuts," I say.

"Can you at least pretend this is an awkward conversation?" Will asks.

Guest Suite

I BUZZ MY FATHER.

"Mr. Whitehall is here to see you," I say.

"I'll be right out," Dad says.

"You can have a seat in the waiting room, Mr. Whitehall," I say. "Would you like coffee, tea, water?"

"Water, please," says Mr. Whitehall.

Wendy ambushes me on my way to the staff kitchen.

"We need to talk," she hisses.

"Okay, what's up?" I say.

"It's not a waiting room," Wendy says.

"What's not a waiting room?" I say.

"The area where people wait," Wendy says.

"I see," I say. "What is the waiting room, then, if it's not 'the area where people wait'?"

"It's to be referred to as the guest suite," Wendy says.

"Is this another Dad-ism, or is this one of your inventions?" I ask.

"Jim and I —let's just say we agree on this," Wendy says.

"People don't like to wait. It makes them feel disrespected. A guest suite sounds welcoming. It has VIP connotations."

"VIP connotations?" I say.

Wendy should have been in government protocol or some rule-based job that would reward her gifts. People are always missing their true callings. They become loyal to the wrong choices.

I carry the bottled water back to Mr. Whitehall.

"Here you go," I say. "I found these Hostess Sno-Balls in the kitchen. And some pretzels, too. Any interest?"

"Sure," says Mr. Whitehall.

I have anticipated his needs, and for that he is appreciative. Food makes waiting seem like a treat. A marshmallow treat, rolled in coconut . . . and dyed shocking pink.

"I hope you're enjoying the guest suite," I say. And its VIP connotations.

"Yes," says Mr. Whitehall.

I walk back into the kitchen. Wendy is waiting for me.

"You just gave away my lunch," Wendy says.

"I know," I say. "I didn't like the way you were talking to me. Do you want me to make you some popcorn or something?" I say.

"Who eats popcorn for lunch?" Wendy says.

Sometimes it seems like we're all just waiting. No matter what you call it.

Grilled Cheese

I'M LEANING AGAINST the counter in her kitchen. My mom looks great. I'm not afraid to say what I need to say, which comes as a shock to me. The therapy is starting to pay off. And my mother doesn't seem fragile anymore.

"I'm thinking it's probably a good time for me to go back to my own place," I say.

"Okay," Mom says. "I was thinking maybe I'd turn your bedroom into a meditation room."

"I had no idea you'd be so broken up about it. Maybe I should stay," I say. "I could sell my place."

"You don't sell in a down market," Mom says.

"It's New York City—there seems to be no such thing," I say.

"I don't feel like cooking. Let's go out for a grilled cheese sandwich," Mom says.

"I don't think restaurants make those anymore. They would cost about a dollar-fifty, and that doesn't seem like enough to justify having waitress service, rent, and so on," I say. "But if you're hungry, I'll make one for you."

"No, no. Let's go out. That place around the corner makes them. They're on the kids' menu," Mom says, with too much authority.

At the corner of Lexington and Eighty-third is a

soda fountain luncheonette that makes grilled cheese sandwiches—for children.

The waitress comes to take our order.

"Grilled cheese and ice water," I say, in hopes of pleasing my mother and making up for the fact that I won't be sleeping over anymore. I've been ordering things I don't want for years, in hopes of pleasing my mother. It never works, but that doesn't stop me from trying.

"I'll have an iced tea," Mom says.

"And she'll have a grilled cheese sandwich, too," I say.

"No, nothing else for me. Just iced tea," Mom says.

"You're not getting a grilled cheese sandwich? That's why we're here," I say. "Is something wrong?"

She's giving me a look.

"I feel fine," Mom says, "I feel great, in fact. I just remembered these people never clean their griddle. I couldn't eat anything off of that filth."

The waitress stands there not knowing what to say.

"But you let me order one?" I say.

"Kids are resilient," Mom says.

"Only because they have to be," I say.

Rest Area

I CAN'T HELP but miss Sam. I love it when I have a dream about him at night, and I can't wait to go back to bed the next night in hopes that I'll dream about him again. I'm living the most exciting part of my life while I'm asleep. It should disturb me more.

I think I see him walking down the sidewalk today. Hope is turning into reality. My chest begins to pound. My conscientious heart is sending me a message—in case my eyes fail—that Sam is near. I walk faster, and finally I am next to him. I look up. It is not Sam.

The disappointment will last all afternoon. I feel a homesickness I did not think was possible at my age.

I stop at a pay phone. I call his home, when he's at work. I want to avoid calling the place I used to work, looking for the man I used to kiss.

"Hello," I say, to his machine. "I just thought I saw you walking in Midtown. I promised myself if it was you I was going to tell you that I've missed you. But it wasn't you."

Escape

IT'S SNOWING. Perry wants to meet for a hot toddy at King's Carriage House. I want to see a movie. We compromise and agree to do both.

"Here's one I've been mulling," Perry says. "I'm thinking of adopting."

"A dog—right?" I ask.

"Dogs are too much work," Perry says. "Maybe I could adopt a teenager. She could run errands and stuff."

"Make sure you mention the errand running during the adoption interview," I say.

"How old do you have to be to know how to balance a checkbook and split wood?" Perry says. "I have a place in Sag Harbor; vines and trees have taken over. The landscaper wanted thirty thousand dollars to remove it. A kid might have fun doing that kind of project."

"Because we all know that teenagers love manual labor," I say. "Anyway, all that yard work will be good practice for the shallow grave she'll eventually be digging for your corpse, Perry."

"You really don't think I should adopt, do you?" Perry says.

"No," I say.

"Yeah, I know," Perry says, his voice trailing off. "Being alone sucks. Do we have to see a movie?" Perry adds.

"What is the resistance to movies?" I say. "We had a deal."

"I'm not a big fan of movies. When I go, I usually go by myself. My father used to take me to the movies all the time when I was a kid. He never planned far enough in advance to get a sitter. I ended up watching some really inappropriate stuff," Perry says.

I'm remembering the car ride home from the Hamptons with Sam. That ridiculous automated navigation system. We talked about movies at the Carlyle.

"That must have been great," I say.

"No. Not really. That was his only escape, and I guess it made me think he was very unimaginative. Or maybe the movies were the adult conversation he missed when he was with me. Hard to know," Perry says.

"I can't imagine a parent being organized enough to select a movie, find a theater, get there on time, and remember to bring money to pay for it—my reference point is so far off from yours. I'd have killed to sit in a theater next to my father," I say.

"And be ignored? The movie wasn't for me; it was his working hard to avoid me," Perry says.

"Or working hard to be next to you," I say. "Working hard not to fight. Working hard to be still, and quiet, and in the same place."

"Never thought of it that way," Perry says.

"Are you on new medication?" I ask.

"That obvious?" Perry says.

"Well, the smart-ass has disappeared for the moment," I say.

"I miss the smart-ass," Perry says.

"Letting go of defenses is never easy. You seem melancholy, but relaxed," I say.

"I know," Perry says. "It feels foreign to me. I hate it." He smiles. "If you were my therapist, I'd tell you this has been one of my favorite sessions ever. It was so true and so all about me."

"Yeah?" I say.

"I never looked at the movies as a chance to be next to someone; I always thought it was avoidance. It seems so obvious now that you've said that," Perry says. "Thanks."

On our second toddy, midsip, I remember my father was supposed to meet me at my apartment. I was going to show him the two-bedroom pride of my existence. Then we were going to order takeout.

I race over to my apartment building almost an hour late.

Holiday Tipping

WHEN IT COMES to holiday tipping, never give homemade baked goods. Always give cash. Select the magic number you are willing to part with, and tack on an additional 10 percent. It will appear very generous. I'm only telling you what I wish someone had told me. Undertipping at Christmastime will catch up with you. Someday. Somewhere. At the place of their choosing.

I look around the lobby; Jim is nowhere to be seen. The doorman appears. It's payback time. I can feel it.

"You looking for your dad?" Federico says.

"Yeah," I say.

"I keyed him into your place. He was sitting here for a while, and he looked beat," Federico says.

"You let him into my apartment?" I ask.

I'm slightly drunk, and sort of giddy. My father is in

my apartment. The doorman let a stranger into my apartment. It occurs to me that I don't even know my father's age. I can guess. But I don't know how old my father is. It seems like the sort of thing a person should know.

My father is sitting on my couch watching TV. His tie is off. He has a bottle of water in one hand and a beer in the other. His boots are sitting by the front door, toes pointing north.

Before I left for work this morning, I looked around my apartment and tried to see what it would look like to someone walking in for the first time. Flowers would help, I remember thinking, but of course I didn't buy any because I'd forgotten my father was coming over.

"Hey, Dad," I say. "You must be pretty smooth to talk your way into my apartment."

"Yes. Very smooth," Jim says.

"Did you eat anything?" I ask.

He must have. My apartment smells like a grease fire. He broiled a steak and didn't use the fan on the stove.

"So, was he a gentleman? Never mind, none of my business," Dad says.

My father has the manners of a man from a different time. He *is* a man from a different time. He was fifteen years older than my mother. When they married, she was twenty-seven. Men can wait to have children. The window of opportunity must seem like some never-ending field of poppies. Just enjoy! Inhale them with your eyes, nose, and every pore. There are so many beautiful flowers. Given such wonderful choices, wouldn't you be required to admire them as a group before you can stand to select just one—and, of course, in his case, he was never able to stick with just one.

"It wasn't a date. I was with a friend," I say. "We lost track of time. Sorry I'm late."

He opens two more beers. We play a game of backgammon. If I had taken the time to buy flowers, I doubt he'd have noticed.

We play two rounds. Then one more round for a tie-breaker. When I sit with him for a while, I always get stuck on the same thing. How did they let it slip away—our family? My family?

My father seems committed to making this last-ditch effort, to rein it all in, give it a tidy ending. He'd be a father who gave his daughter a job; he'd be the kind of guy who would visit his ailing ex-wife. It all just seems so sad and full of regret. Yet he doesn't seem sad; he seems rather content.

"What would you do differently? If reliving your life were possible?" I ask.

"Where do I start? I would have worked harder to make a life with your mom. Yet I'm not sure working harder would have changed anything. But allowing that relationship to fail, especially the way it failed—with you girls and so on," Dad says.

I'm picturing a dam giving way, and things around it

collapsing. The water's reach is farther than you could ever expect.

"Thanks for waiting up for me, Dad," I say. I don't say that I've always wanted to have a father wait up for me. "I'm sorry I was so late."

Fake Accent

I CALL MARJORIE because I come across a piece of paper that has her name and number on it, and I remember I'm supposed to call her, but I don't remember why I'm supposed to call. Because we're sisters? Because she's recently had a baby and people who have babies lose touch with people who don't have babies?

A woman with a rich European accent answers the phone. I'm thinking it has to be the baby nurse. Marjorie must be at the gym with her personal trainer, making her postbaby body even better than her prebaby body. But I thought the latest baby nurse was a quiet Colombian woman (a perk to hiring her, according to Marjorie, was that she didn't understand a word of English and therefore could not eavesdrop). This seemed like an odd consideration, as Marjorie has a track record that demonstrates little need for secrets.

"Doesn't that mean she also can't communicate with Poison Control?" I ask, concerned this hadn't occurred to Marjorie in her postnatal haze.

"You're such a worrier!" Marjorie says.

The woman answering the phone sounds as if she might be European royalty, though from what country she's spawned I cannot determine.

"Halo?" says this refined voice.

"May I please speak with Marjorie?" I ask.

Extremely long pause follows. Possibly she's inhaling a cigarette. Blowing adorable smoke rings into the baby's face?

"Hey, Em, it's me," Marjorie says.

"Oh?" I say. "What's with the accent?"

If I hadn't asked the question, my sister would not have explained herself and would in fact have pretended she hadn't answered the phone in a foreign dialect. She is my mother's daughter so much more than I could *ever* be my mother's daughter.

"Oh, I'm dodging our super," Marjorie says.

"You're a grown woman—you have a baby," I say.

"Don't sound disappointed. It's judgmental. Besides, you *know* I'm crazy," Marjorie says.

"Right. The proof just keeps on piling up," I say. "I thought all of that would change when you became a mother. But you're able to produce a staggering amount of horseshit."

"God gives everyone a unique gift," Marjorie says.

"What did you do to the super? Or do I not want to know?" I ask.

"I saw a cockroach," Marjorie says.

"Yes?" I say. It's New York City.

"I freaked out on his answering machine," Marjorie says. "Actually, I was still kind of drunk this morning and overreacted. I had a real harpy rant: 'What if it goes after the baby? You're responsible if it chases my precious son,'" Marjorie says, laughing.

"The super? Or the cockroach?" I ask. "Never mind, but I think you might be right about the baby nurse," I say, remembering what I was supposed to call her about.

"Of course I'm right about the baby nurse—she really is a better mother than I could ever be," Marjorie reasons.

Excellent point. Yet if you can see your deficiencies so clearly, can't you correct them?

"Thanks for checking in," Marjorie says. "But I'm in a hurry. I'm about to meet Dory at Swiss Chalet; we're headed to St. Moritz, and I have a tire around my belly—and my ass—and I need some new ski clothing and some cigarettes."

Dory is back on the payroll. She also has Marjorie on a strict postpregnancy diet of lemon water and cigarettes.

"Oh, okay. Who's watching Malcolm while you're away?" I ask.

"Baby nurse," Marjorie says. "Unless you want to watch him."

How did Marjorie pick and choose which of our

mother's personality quirks to keep in her version of motherhood? And how did she decide which odd behaviors should be replaced to create her own unique spin on raising a baby?

I hang up the phone. I imagine what kind of mother I'd be. I sometimes think motherhood might expose some of my better qualities. Patience. Affection. Storytelling. Why is it easier for me to imagine having a baby than having a relationship with Sam? I'm fantasizing about a relationship that doesn't allow me to have one foot out the door. That's a first.

Doctor/Patient Relationships

HE'S ALL MINE. Except that he's also the woman's whose appointment is just before mine (head cast down, looks like she could be blown over by a strong gust of wind, but still pretty in a bookish way, which is a quality I suspect he'd really like). I hope for my sake he doesn't have to listen to her tales of sexual dysfunction. I hope instead it's something he wouldn't secretly find kind of appealing. Pyromania, for example.

She and I have something in common—which is scary. We're both kind of in love with Paul. I can tell by the way she leaves his office looking so territorial and reluctant. I remain forever grateful that I don't have to see the parade of his patients and measure myself against each one of them.

"What are you thinking?" Paul asks.

"Ask again later," I say.

He waits a beat. "What are you thinking?" Paul asks again.

"I'd tell you, but you'd mock me," I say.

"Mocking people can be very entertaining," Paul says.

I consider it. I've had this question ricocheting around my brain for a few weeks now; when I was close to asking it, I'd wise up. It's a test: I want to see if he'll lie or tell the truth. Testing people is a terrible thing, and it's my compulsion.

"Okay," I say. "Okay. Okay . . . yeah. Um, would you ever . . . hit on me? Like at a party or something?" I ask.

He smiles. "Patient-doctor relationships aren't ethical," Paul says.

"If it were ethical, it'd hardly be exciting," I say. Nitwit! "What I'm saying is, what if I wasn't your patient? Pretend we're total strangers and we meet at a party—then, would you hit on me?"

"Meeting you at a cocktail party—I'd be thinking that I'm twenty years older than you," Paul says.

"And to your thinking that's a good thing or a bad thing?" I say.

He smiles.

"Okay, we're at a party, and I'm offering sex, no strings attached?" I say.

"It would be rude to say no to that," Paul says.

I'm satisfied with this. I've begged the guy to hypothetically consider sleeping with me. And *I'm* satisfied? But he's not.

"The truth is, I'd be more likely to 'hit on you' in real life. I know you. At a party, you'd just be one more person," Paul says.

"You'd really hit on me?" I say incredulously. "You might want to investigate that self-destructive streak before the inquest. I like you. I really do. But I will not lie under oath."

My conversations with him are always directed at the wrong person. I need to transfer this longing back where it belongs. To Sam. As safe as it is, I can't keep hitting on my shrink.

"I just realized what I've been doing," I say. "I need to call Sam."

"Good," Paul says. "Are you going to?"

"Eventually," I say. "We both know I like to put off the things that are good for me."

"I've noticed. I wasn't sure you had," Paul says.

"Yeah. Mammogram . . . Sam . . ." I say.

Finding Religion

IT'S EIGHT-THIRTY on Sunday morning. I'm running out of the park, and walk over to Madison to pick up a post-jog latte to simulate that runner's high I've heard so much about. I see Marjorie. She looks great. If this were a year ago, I'd assume she was dressed from the night before, and picking up a bagel on her way home to sleep it off. In the way that my mother is a morning person, my sister is the polar opposite.

"Hey!" I call.

"Hey, sweetie," Marjorie says.

"You look great," I say.

"It's the microdermabrasion. My cheeks feel like a baby's ass. And the spa offers child care!" Marjorie says, smiling. "Well, off to church!"

"Right," I say, wink-wink, *"off to church."*

"Seriously," Marjorie says.

"No," I say. "No. I thought 'church' was code for 'sleep off hangover.' I'm surprised to see you awake and dressed."

"That's what happens when you have a baby. Besides, we've found the Lord," Marjorie says. "Who knew he'd be attending the city's hottest nursery school? We have to be model citizens for two years 'til he's in. We're greeters today."

"Doesn't Little Malcolm have legacy status at at least two nursery schools?" I ask.

"Oh, honey, the world has changed. We need a safety school," Marjorie says.

Marjorie has a baby, someone else to consider, and I don't. I do, of course—my mother. She is my emotional seat-filler. She gets to be the most important person in my

life until I get more courage and put an end to this pro-
crastination.

Marjorie doesn't know where her child will be admitted to nursery school to play with blocks, meet tiny friends,
and nap on linoleum. And she's apparently so consumed
by it she's willing to greet people on the steps of the church
on Sunday morning. Not bad for someone who would fail
the simplest of drug tests.

I'm a lawyer. I can mount a defense for my procrasti-
nation. I mailed a postcard to Sam. I left a message for
him just before my pizza date with Will. In each case, he
didn't respond. I saw him having lunch with, gasp, a
woman. When I called from the hospital, he was entertaining. These are all great reasons never to contact him
again. Except they're actually not a defense at all but a
string of pathetic excuses. Why would he respond to a
postcard? All that postcard told him was that I haven't
learned anything. I reach out from a distance. I keep myself planted safely far away. No risk. No return.

The Things We Do for Love

I'M IN THE KITCHEN at the office. I am opening the
fridge to put some milk away when I notice how out of order the whole inside is. I've seen the same yogurt in there
for at least two weeks. I start tossing things out quickly, as
if they are bombs about to explode. It's very satisfying.
The riddance of things we don't need.

My father walks in. He puts a coffee cup in the sink. He looks inside the cabinet where we keep the trash bags. Then he looks over his shoulder, then back at the cabinet. He grabs several handfuls of small wastebasket-sized trash bags and shuffles them into the box of tall kitchen bags. There is some obvious muscle memory happening here—it's all very slick and practiced.

"Why do you do that?" I ask.

"What?" Dad says.

"Mess up all the trash bags and mix the different sizes together," I say.

He considers whether he should tell the truth or pretend I am mistaken about what I just saw.

"So she knows I'm thinking about her," Dad says.

"Why not just tell Wendy you're thinking about her?" I say.

"It's not how we do things," Dad says.

I always thought my parents communicated on the indirect plane because they didn't know how else to communicate. I was half right. My mother never knew how to communicate, and my father was willing to live in her world and learn her strange language. The language rooted in strange acts of intimacy and no direct conversations whatsoever. They'd live happily if the world was an impressionist painting, not a realist painting. The same language he's using to seduce the fair Wendy.

Sharp Right Turn

WE'RE SEATED AT his table at the Club. It's been several months since our first lunch here. There is a comfort in our routine. Every Friday: lunch, drinks, chat.

"This is nice, isn't it?" Dad says.

He reaches for my hand and squeezes it.

"Yes," I say.

It is nice. No wonder I felt like a stranger growing up in my mother's house. My emotional compass more closely resembles my father's than my mother's.

He is eating a Cobb salad. He takes a sip of his martini.

He waves Martin the waiter over to the table.

"Marty, this doesn't taste good to me today. I'll have a wine spritzer," Dad says.

"Right away, Mr. Rhode," Martin says. He dashes off with the subpar beverage in hand. He moves swiftly, as if handing off a baton in a relay race.

"A spritzer? Kind of a girl drink, don't you think?" I say.

"Maybe so," my father says, disconnected. Not playing along. "Maybe so."

He takes a prescription bottle out of his jacket pocket. He puts a pill in his mouth and taps his fingers on the table. Because he's discovered that tapping his fingers ushers the medication into his bloodstream more quickly? The color drains out of his face.

"Are you okay?" I ask.

"I'm not sure," Dad says.

"Have some more water," I say. "Do you want me to get you to a doctor?"

He taps his fingers on the table again.

"Emily, don't . . ." Dad says.

"Don't what?" I ask.

He slumps forward in slow motion, and I am frozen in my chair. Then I stand up just as his head and shoulders land on the table.

"Dad!? Help!" I say loudly, or yell, I'm not quite sure. Is there anyone else in the room? Are they all still eating? I don't know. Because I can't take my eyes off of my father. His body resting heavily in front of me.

Within seconds Martin and another waiter have him laid out on the floor. They perform CPR. Paramedics arrive.

An adrenaline shot is given. He seems to revive and sit almost upright for a few seconds, only to collapse again. At the Club and in the ambulance, they spend close to an hour trying to convince his heart to restart.

Don't save the grand gestures for the end, I keep thinking. Just don't do it. You might die tomorrow; you might not. But avoid your family and then try to catch up at the very end, and life just won't allow it.

I Need Order

WHAT ARE YOU supposed to do when someone dies? First order of business, I'm guessing, is to forget all about "supposed to." Perhaps forget about "supposed to" for forever, in fact. These are the lessons you learn in those pivotal moments.

I'm sitting at my desk in my apartment. I took a cab home but I don't remember the ride. I notice some smudges on the phone, and can't help but clean it. Wendy taught me this. Always clean the phone, and you'll almost never get the cold that's going around. When I lift the receiver to use the phone, I smell Aqua Velva. He must have used this phone that night he got keyed into my apartment.

I call my mom to tell her the news.

"Dad is dead," I say.

"Jim is dead?" Mom asks.

"Yes," I say.

"I'll come right over," Mom says. "You make some tea."

"Okay," I say.

That stupid jerk, I keep thinking. He's dead. Popsicles for breakfast. "I'm a bachelor." Childish jerk.

I don't make tea. I don't move from where I'm seated at my desk. He's gone again.

My mom arrives. She has a shopping bag. She's always prepared, always looking for reasons to shop.

"You haven't been home much in the past few months," Mom says. "I thought you might need some things."

"You're right. Thanks," I say.

"What happened?" Mom says.

"We were having lunch. He had a heart attack," I say.

"You were there?" Mom asks.

I nod. I can't say the word yes without crying.

My mother starts crying. I start crying.

"I'm just so . . . mad. I'm so mad at him," I say. "I can't help it. I'm just furious. What the hell was he waiting for these past twenty years? You wouldn't believe the way people treat him at work. They adore him. I was starting to adore him. They have no idea we've barely seen each other for the last twenty years."

My mother hugs me. She doesn't know what to say.

"I'm really going to miss him," I say. "I've always missed him."

Divine Bar Snacks

I'M SUPPOSED TO MEET Perry for dinner. I can't bear the thought of having to talk tonight. I can't bear the thought of staying home alone. Marjorie is skiing, so she's not an option.

"Phil's coming over tonight to watch a movie. Join us," Mom says.

Really? Phil can't take a rain check for one night? My father is *dead*!

"I had plans to meet Perry," I say. "I guess I'll just keep them."

"I'll tell you what, you can choose the movie," Mom says.

"It's not about the movie," I say.

Perry and I meet at the Carlyle in the Café. The waiter comes to the table and places snacks and drink menus on the table.

"We'll have two glasses of the same smack that couple is having," Perry says.

"Red wine?" the waiter asks.

"Yes," Perry says. The waiter walks away.

"This place has got the most divine bar snacks," Perry says. "This silver snack caddy makes me feel good about eating salted nuts. Not the cheap nuts, either. Not peanuts. The good nuts. Macadamias, pistachios. They wouldn't think of serving something we had to shell ourselves. P.S. What the hell happened to you? You look like your dog died."

"My father," I say.

"Yeah? What about Jim? What crazy life lesson are you extrapolating from being his receptionist this week?" Perry asks, throwing back a handful of nuts.

"My father died," I say.

There is an audible gasp.

It gets more real each minute. He's dead.

"I am just so humiliated. I can't believe that you let me go on and on about salted snacks," Perry says.

How often do you get a second chance? Every day.

How often do you take the second chance? Almost never. Things were kind of odd and extraordinary while they lasted.

Eulogy

IT'S A MISTAKE to wait until someone dies to eulogize him. It's too late.

I sit at my desk not knowing what to write. This letter is for me, not him. I don't want to leave things left unsaid. I don't want to forget how I feel this time.

Dear Dad,

> *Most of my life when I've thought about you, I've felt some vague pity for you and for what you've missed—seeing Marjorie and me grow up.*
>
> *It's only after spending time with you that I've realized it was easier to imagine what you were missing out on, because it was too painful to imagine what I was missing. I was just getting to know you. Things were just starting to become more clear to me.*
>
> *I'll miss the formality in your voice when we shared a cab in the morning, and the way you called the cabdriver "sir." I'll miss listening in on your phone calls and eavesdropping on your relationship with Wendy.*
>
> *Your desertion was part of you, but it wasn't all of you. And what I've learned about you, I've really liked.*

When we had lunch at the Club that first day, you told me you never knew your father. I guess we had a lot in common. There have been surprises every day that I've known you, but what surprised me the most was that you were knowable. *A few months ago, you were a mystery.*

I can't help wonder if the past six months will slip away and turn into a mirage. Your return, my job as the receptionist, our lunches at the Club, your taste in wacky socks, and your polite lack of interest in my love life . . . When I was five and you left, I forgot what it was like to have a father. I grew up making myself forget. I don't want to forget this time.

Funeral Food

MY MOTHER HAS always loved parties. She can control what people eat, what they see, what they drink . . . and at the same time transform her dining room into a circus tent or planetarium.

"I think it's a good idea to have people come back here after the service," Mom says. She is remarkably calm.

"Yes," I say. "I think so, too. Do we have this catered? What do we do?" I ask.

"Oh, you let me take care of that," Mom says.

What wasn't in the form of a casserole was in the form of a ball. This being the only way to describe the food served after my father's funeral.

Within a week of my mother's diagnosis, she started interviewing caterers for her own postfuneral luncheon. She wanted the theme to be "whimsy" and for people to feel "happy" that she had lived. Out of guilt for making a full recovery, she hired the same caterers for my father's funeral—but slashed the budget in half.

"It only seems fair to hire them," Mom says. "After that show they put on with canapé tasting and wine pairings. That was positively embarrassing. I had to hire them after that."

The caterers seemed more than a little relieved that *someone* had died.

Marjorie opted to boycott this gathering in my father's honor. Most of my life I've resented that the rules were different for her than for me. I guess I never considered how much you might miss if you're always given the option to opt out.

I considered borrowing some Xanax from my mother's medicine cabinet to get through the day. I decided against it because it seems a lot like sweeping dirt from one part of a room to another. You can make it disappear from your line of vision temporarily, but at some point you just have to deal with it. Now is that time.

Will puts his arm around me. He kisses my cheek.

"I'm going to miss him," Will says. "He was a good man."

"Yes," I say. "He was."

"And a maniac on the squash court," Will says.

Wendy walks into the living room. We should have let her plan this. She's an excellent coordinator. Den mother. She's holding what looks like a piña colada. There is an umbrella in it.

"Is that a piña colada?" I ask.

"I've been here twenty minutes, and it's my second one," Wendy says. "Jim would have loved this."

Wendy is wearing black. Her eyes are teary and puffy, and she's obviously been crying off and on since Friday. She will miss my father more than most other people in this room today. That's the tricky part about life. Where is Wendy going to meet my father's replacement? The man she can love but stay distantly safe from? She's cultivated her ideal relationship for fifteen years, and she's only forty. Where will she meet another man she's tempted to confess her love to on a daily basis because if he dies tomorrow, she'd wish she had? Does she wake up every morning wishing she'd confessed her love for him? Wondering what might have happened? Will she have to break form and find a new kind of love? Am I talking about Wendy or myself? Or a combination of the two?

"Especially the umbrellas. It's a cute idea," Wendy says.

"Seems oddly festive, doesn't it?" I say.

"Why shouldn't it be? He was a really happy guy," Wendy says.

She's right. He was. I'm relieved she remembers him as a "happy guy."

"I know that you meant a lot to him," I say.

Wendy eyes me suspiciously. Hopefully.

"It was obvious," I say.

"Was it?" Wendy asks. Tears roll down her cheeks.

"Yes," I say, hugging her.

Perry walks toward me. He hugs me, and the hug feels like it arrived just in time. Like it is the only thing keeping me standing on two feet.

"The bartender is serving mud slides. Is there any chance they confused this with a bachelorette party?" Perry asks.

"Thanks for coming," I say.

"Well, if it's a bachelorette party, there's the guy I want to see in the G-string," Perry says.

I look in the general direction of his lust. It's Sam.

I pegged Sam wrong. I thought he was the sort of person who would require an invitation to a funeral. He certainly wouldn't show up without knowing he was welcome. Except that he did.

"Sam," I say, quietly to myself.

His being there is more important to me than I would have imagined. And that makes me cry again.

When I see Sam there, in our living room, I don't go over to say "hello." Saying "hello" might be the permission he needs to leave. His appearance will have served its purpose.

Mostly I remember the whole event seeming like some

sort of advertisement for meatballs. You manage not to see ball-shaped food for a good portion of your life, then suddenly you're surrounded by it. There are Swedish meatballs, turkey spheres, crab balls, and for the oft-ignored vegetarian funeralgoer, orb-shaped food made of cheese and also saffron risotto.

Nana is seated at a table near the front door. When people walk by her, she asks if they've signed the guest book. There is a line for a signature, and a line for a comment or greeting. No one can muster a greeting. So instead we have a record of attendance.

I go to my mother's bedroom to find Nana's coat. As she slips it on, I notice she smells like mothballs. We'll all be old someday.

"My fur has that awful mothball smell, doesn't it?" Nana asks.

"Oh, thank God it's your coat," I say.

"Excuse me?" Nana says.

"I'm sorry," I say. I never will get the knack of grieving gracefully.

I sit down on the bed. I decide to take a nap, right there on top of a soft sea of coats belonging to my parents' friends and acquaintances for the past thirty years. I'm not sure how long I'm out before I am awakened.

"There you are," Sam says. "Too many meatballs?"

"Too many people," I say, sitting up.

"Don't move," Sam says.

He turns out the one dimmed light in the room. He lies

down next to me. And kisses my forehead. It's not enough. I kiss his lips, his neck. I pull him to me, on top of me.

"I've missed you," I say.

"I can tell," Sam says. "I've missed you, too."

My Father

I CLEANED OUT his stuff. I did his closets, because when Wendy tried, she broke down. She did the fridge, the kitchen cabinets, the impersonal stuff.

It's not clear if she's crying because she's being flooded with regret over what could have been, or if she's so moved to be included in the decision making and chores usually left to a wife. Either way, my sister Marjorie would not help me, so I called Wendy because I knew she'd be careful with his belongings. Maybe a little too careful. She treats every dish as if it were a piece of pre-revolutionary porcelain.

His closet is an archaeological find. In the back of the long closet were the suits he hadn't worn in years, the earliest layer of history. There is a tennis sweater that might have even been from his college days. I have a vague recollection of it. But it's vague enough not to be true. He is a paper doll, and I've dressed him in my head, in each suit in this closet. Fact: His waist grew from size 36 to 38 to 40, and then down to 36 again. His heart wanted more than that, apparently.

There is a wooden tray covered in felt. Cuff links sit there tarnishing, not knowing he's dead.

When you don't know what you're searching for, it's hard to know you've found it. There's no eureka moment. It's hard to determine what was important among the wallpaper of gray suits.

In the back of his closet, in a plain cardboard box, I discover the strata that I must have been looking for. My secret goal. Not Jurassic, but early Emily. There is a yellowed tissue paper–covered bundle, inside which is a ceramic Santa Claus mug. The kind that has Santa's whole face on it. His beard is chipped, and on the brim of Santa's hat in gold paint it says "Emily." There is one belonging to Marjorie, too.

We used to leave the mug out for Santa Claus on Christmas Eve, with a plate of cookies, and he'd dutifully drink the milk, and eat the cookies, and leave a massive pile of gifts as thanks for the snack. I always felt I was getting the better end of the deal.

There are paper chains made of faded construction paper. There is still some glitter stuck to the paper chains, but most of it has fallen off. There were other homemade wooden ornaments, hand-painted, that I vaguely remembered.

At the bottom of this treasure trove is a shoe box. Inside were some black-and-white photos of my father. Some from high school. Some from the air force. There was a photo of my mother in Central Park holding Marjorie while pregnant with me. Another one of me sitting next to Marjorie. I look like I'm about two.

I think you can measure a family's happiness by how many photos they take. They want to capture the feeling on film, because they are buoyant enough to believe capturing happiness is possible.

All of the evidence of his marriage was neatly stored in one brown box. He was working as hard on forgetting as I was. We were very much alike.

Marking Time

IT'S HARD NOT to see things as beginnings and endings. When someone dies, you want to mark time before or after . . . but time is time. It's a continuous motion, and we divide it into increments to pretend to have some control over it. To make it neat and manageable.

My mother has been reminiscing.

"The first time I held his hand, it fit," Mom says.

My mother has told me this before. But I always assumed this was my mother's delicate euphemism for sex. Now I'm pretty sure she's actually been talking about handholding the entire time.

"It didn't just fit, it fit perfectly. Your father was a fascinating man. No one could forget him," Mom says.

"You really loved him at some point, didn't you?" I ask.

"You don't live with someone for ten years and have children and manage to not be in love. It's not possible," Mom says.

"That's what I figured," I say.

"I want to talk to you about something," Mom says.

"What?" I say.

The familiar sinking sensation comes over me. Don't let the cancer be back. Is this how I'm going to feel forever? Every time she tells me she needs to talk to me?

"A few months ago we were talking and you said you couldn't remember when your father lived with us," Mom says.

"Yeah?" I say.

"There's something you should know," Mom says. "I left your father."

"You mean you kicked him out?" I say.

"No. We had an argument, and I left. I was gone for four weeks. I left you here," Mom says.

"Why did you leave?" I ask.

"There was no reason good enough, Emily. I left because I'd had it with your father . . . and his friends. Girlfriends. I was tired of wondering where he was. Maybe I wanted him to wonder where I was for a change. It was childish," Mom says.

"Oh. But you left . . . me?" I ask. "Not both of us? Not me and Marjorie?"

My mother sits and stares for a while.

"No. Not Marjorie. You adored him. I thought you'd miss him more than you'd miss me," Mom says.

"Did you also think his extracurricular activities

would be hindered by having a five-year-old to care for?"
I say.

"Some part of me must have," Mom says.

I hate her for answering that question honestly, and I
respect her for answering that question.

"Where did you and Marjorie go?" I ask.

"To my mother's house," Mom says.

"That's why you and Nana stopped speaking?" I say.

"She's never been able to forgive me for leaving you,"
Mom says. "The truth is if it wasn't that, it would have
been something else. Oil and water don't mix."

"Neither do insanity and child rearing," I say. "Did I
really prefer him that much?"

"Yes, you and he were a lot alike," Mom says. "I mean
his good qualities, Emily. He could be very empathetic.
But he was frightened of being close to people. That's what
led to all of those women. It's not something either one of
us was prepared to work on."

Affairs

IT WASN'T ONE WOMAN. It wasn't something in the moment that I can romanticize away as one true love; it was
many women. She knew. My mother knew about the other
women. He knew she knew, yet could never bring himself
to tell her the truth. And she didn't hate him, so I started
to hate him for her. I did what she refused to do.

But nothing is ever what it seems to be, because you can never see the back while you're looking at the front, or the top while you're looking at the bottom. One side, that's mostly what you get. Especially if you're living with one of the sides, and that side is the one who is making you dinner, and checking your homework, and doing the job of two people.

Date Book

THERE WAS A DATE BOOK that he'd kept. The old-fashioned kind, the kind you write in with a pencil. He had a dentist appointment booked three weeks after his death. As a courtesy—okay, out of curiosity I went to the appointment.

"Hi, my father was Jim Rhode," I say. "He died a few weeks ago. So I thought maybe I'd take his appointment."

"Oh," the receptionist says. "Well, you'll need to fill out a new patient form."

She hands me a clipboard. I fill out the paperwork. I'm escorted into Dr. Johnson's work area. A few minutes later she appears.

Dr. Johnson is the prettiest dentist I've ever seen. She's wearing a black skirt, and she's tall. She has horn-rimmed glasses, and a white dentist-type jacket. Black pumps.

"I'm so sorry, Michele told me Jim died. He seemed so . . . full of life," Dr. Johnson says.

Oh my God, my father slept with his dentist, too. He must have. There's no way he wouldn't have at least tried.

"Yes. Well, it was very sudden," I say. "Anyway, I had my teeth cleaned about two months ago, but I'll go again. You can never make them too clean. Although some people are going a little nuts making them too white. Have you noticed how people's teeth actually glow now? It's disturbing."

I sit in the big chair. Dr. Johnson puts the enormous paper bib on me. She moves the chair into the reclining position.

"Open," Dr. Johnson says.

She peers inside my mouth and pokes around with some stainless steel tools.

"Your father had quick buildup of plaque, too," Dr. Johnson says.

"Really?" I say.

Another gem I'd never known about him. It makes me miss him. Tears form in my eyes.

"How long did you know him?" I ask.

"He was a handoff from Dr. Kramer, so I'd say I've known your father nine or ten years."

"What was he like?"

"He refused X-rays, and avoided us as much as he could," Dr. Johnson says.

"Hmm," I say. "Don't most people avoid X-rays and dentists?"

"Yes, I guess it's pretty universal," Dr. Johnson says. "Oh, and he did take antibiotics before cleanings because he had a heart murmur. That was pretty much it."

I pay the receptionist. She hands me some forms to submit to my insurance company. I'm not even sure I have dental insurance anymore. Dr. Johnson walks into the reception area. She watches me put my jacket on.

"I'm very sorry about your father," Dr. Johnson says.

"Thank you," I say. "Can I ask you something kind of personal?"

"Okay, but I may not answer the question," Dr. Johnson says.

"Did he ever ask you out?" I say.

"We had a few dates," Dr. Johnson says.

I knew it!

"Did he seem happy?" I ask. "Not on the dates, just in general? Did he seem happy to you?"

"He seemed satisfied," Dr. Johnson says.

Almost Home

I STOP AND BUY a succulent plant. Don't know why exactly, it seems like a manly plant. I had choices. Green grass in a wooden crate. An orchid. Or this succulent plant. Anything but funeral flowers.

The doorman looks at me without a hint of recognition. Why should there be? We didn't spend much time at Sam's. We didn't spend much time at all. We were planning to. Still, if he'd looked at me with any familiarity, I could have relaxed. I could have felt almost home.

"I'm here to see Sam in 12A," I say.

"Name?" the doorman asks.

"Emily," I say.

He speaks into a phone. Nods his head. "Go on up," the doorman says.

"Oh, I don't want to go up, I wanted to go for a walk," I say.

"Oh. Well, you have to take the plant up, right?" the doorman says.

"Right," I say. The plant was the excuse to get through his front door. My shopping subconscious knew this. The doorman knew this. Yet, I am gleefully oblivious—without actually being gleeful.

Sam opens the door. He's wearing jeans and an old button-down.

"Hey," Sam says.

I hand him the plant, as if it explains everything.

"What's this?" Sam says.

"A plant," I say.

"Yes, I see. For what?" Sam says.

"For you," I say.

"Why?" Sam says.

"I don't know. Because it's easier than just asking if I

can come in," I say. "Can't you just take the plant and stop asking the questions?"

"Okay," Sam says.

"Should we go for a walk?" I ask.

"You just got here. Why are we running out the door?" Sam says. "Would you like something?"

"Sure, the ability to be comforted by another human being without living in terror would be nice. Or, if you have water, I'd take that, too," I say.

"I'm not sure I should make this easy for you," Sam says.

Science

WE ARE LYING IN BED.

"Run while you still can," I say.

"What now?" Sam says.

"Sometimes—I practice being blind," I say.

"That's normal," Sam assures me. "Everyone does that. Just don't do it while you're driving."

"Does everyone know it takes twenty-one steps to get from my apartment door to my elevator? Fifty-two steps from lobby to curb? That to correctly push the button for the twenty-third floor, one can measure two hand lengths, plus the tip of my pinky, just to the first knuckle? Sometimes I panic because I realize I haven't measured every scenario I will encounter."

"So you'll need some help," Sam says, "if you ever do go blind."

"Yes," I say. "That's what makes me panic."

"That would make anyone panic," Sam says. "Even if she were prepared."

"That's one of my favorite things about you," I say.

"What?" Sam says.

"The way you entertain my hypotheticals . . . but not too much," I say.

When he falls asleep, I perform experiments on him. Nothing too invasive. No amateur angioplasty. I try to avoid actions that will get me apprehended.

He breathes heavily, until his breathing becomes snoring . . . I lightly, barely even touching him, put one finger on his arm. He stops snoring. His breathing slows. I wait a minute. I remove my finger. Slowly, his breathing turns into snoring again. I do this over and over again, each time touching him for a different length of time. Each time, my touching stops his snoring—it calms him down—even though he's not conscious of being touched. That kind of trickery would never work on me.

I actually have started to cry several times, sitting cross-legged next to him as he sleeps. I've started to cry thinking about his death. It's disturbing for all sorts of reasons: mainly, because he's perfectly healthy albeit an impressive snorer. I remind myself that Sam has never left me. I left Sam.

I review the data. I touch his arm lightly, his snoring stops. I lift my hand from his skin, and he snores again. In repeated trials I get the same result. The study reveals that he is consistent, and that I am troubled.

He Whose Name Cannot Be Spoken

I'M IN PERRY'S KITCHEN talking about Christmas shopping. I recognize it's a real breakthrough that I am looking forward to celebrating Christmas again. That because of Sam this holiday will be an unspoiled one. At the same time, this realization is at odds with my sudden urge to run out on Perry.

"I'm swimming in debt," he's saying hysterically. "It's not even my debt. He used my credit cards. He paid half of our mortgage. I'm stuck with all of this. On top of that, he's been dead for seventeen months, and I'm still paying off his hospital bills."

"Cancer isn't cheap," I say.

"Roger didn't have cancer," Perry snaps. "He had HIV. It's just such a cliché. I hate it. And I hate it that I'm embarrassed by how he died. Why couldn't he have died of a heart attack like your dad? That's so American it's patriotic."

I'd love to ask Perry what combo of drugs he's on. But I have a feeling that he's not on any medication, that he's finally dealing with the stuff he didn't deal with when Roger died. Instead he kept us all at arm's length, even lying about the diagnosis, I'm stunned to find out, and started opening more T-shirt shops.

"I'm proud of you for getting to the stuff about Roger. Not that you need me to be proud of you or anything," I say.

He was always hiding behind the mythical combination of drugs that would cure loss. His pharmacologist had become Oz.

I don't remember much fighting. Except for one fight. It happened on Christmas Eve. I was probably four.

My father had come home from work late. My mother called his office. She called his friends. She couldn't track him down. She snapped at me. I remember thinking, at that young age, that my mother wasn't worried—she was mad.

Just before I went to bed, he arrived home. My mother met him at the apartment door. He greeted her with a huge smile and said he'd been out shopping all day—looking for the perfect gift, for the perfect wife.

She opened a small box and pulled out a pearl and gold bracelet. She didn't swoon, or melt. She looked at the bracelet, then looked at my father. She handed him the bracelet and said: "Take it back to whomever it belongs to."

He tried to convince her this bracelet was for her. She pointed to some dents in the gold.

"I don't know where you got this. I don't know if I want to know where you got this. But this is not my bracelet!" she yelled.

My mother was not a yeller. Not really, anyway. She could scream as good as the next mom. But mostly she bottled it up, and it came out at inappropriate times. This time, though, she couldn't.

I was afraid of Christmas after that. Worried what my father might drag home. Worried my mother wouldn't save up her anger. That was the last Christmas we had as a family.

The Heart

UNTIL PERRY MENTIONED my father's heart attack, I hadn't given the specifics of it much thought. I was busy absorbing the shock that he was dead. It felt good at the funeral finally to have everyone's pity and prayers. At last I was getting the sympathy I deserved when I was five years old and he left. I'll admit, the condolences I received only left me wanting more.

For months after he died I reread the sympathy cards. Printed proof of my loss, and that the world knew something had been taken from me.

I have an urgent need to understand what actually happened inside of him, to him. Is the heart as unforgiving as a human? Does it turn on its master?

It's just a muscle the size of your fist, but it runs the whole show. It can pump a gallon and a half of blood per minute, while resting. The production requires the complete effort of the whole team. The atria, the aorta, the superior vena cava, the valves, the ventricles, the arteries—they're all there, plugging away every day, all the time. No loafing. No time for hobbies. Or families. A thankless job. And it takes only one of them to go on strike to shut down the whole factory. Which one of them gave up, I wondered, on my dad? What part of me might quit first? Who would feel my loss the most?

Christmas Tree Lights

WE BUY THE TREE on the corner of Seventy-ninth and Madison. Some Boy Scouts are selling them. For five dollars they haul it home and into the apartment. It's a very Norman Rockwell way to get a tree in New York City. Who delivers anything for five dollars?

We have a large bread knife that we are using to shave the trunk of the tree so that it will fit into the stand. We take turns doing the sawing. Then hoist the tree into the stand, and slide it into the corner.

"I know what you can get me for Christmas," Sam says, breathing heavily.

"What?" I ask.

"You can get me someone to put the Christmas lights on the tree," Sam says.

"Chores? You want someone to do your chores for Christmas?" I ask. "And you want your gift *before* Christmas. That's just not right." Besides, I was envisioning something that could be wrapped up very nicely.

"But it's what I want," Sam says. "What do you want?"

"I don't know," I say.

"Gotta be something," Sam says.

Well, sure. There's always something. It's just a question of whether you have the courage to say the *something*.

"So, what do you want?" Sam asks.

"A baby," I say.

"A baby?" Sam says. "I thought you were going to say jewelry."

Leather Coat Christmas

I SPEND VERY LITTLE time thinking about the perfect gift for Sam. Instead, I believe the perfect gift will appear, and by doing so will obviously present itself as the right choice. By December 23, that does not happen. I experience some panic. Should I have planned something weeks ago while planning was still a possibility?

I go to Bergdorf's to find something overpriced to prove my love. What is the perfect gift for the person who makes me believe, really believe, that it's possible to work through things? That leaving is the last resort, not the first? I want to give him something big and unnecessary to properly thank him. So I buy him, of all things, a leather coat.

On Christmas Eve, he opens some champagne. Builds a fire. We're opening some gifts. He's more of a suede coat guy—but I don't realize this until he's about to open the leather coat. And then, too late, it seems so obviously wrong for him.

He unwraps the box. Opens it and holds up the coat. He's stumped.

"A leather coat?" Sam says.

"I'm taking it back," I say.

"I'll be a tough guy in this, huh?" Sam says.

"Put it back in the box," I say.

"No, I'm a tough guy. I'm getting a tattoo. I'm a tough guy," Sam says, walking around in the leather coat. "Look at me, I'm tough, I wear black leather. That can mean only one thing. . . ."

"You're a tough guy?" I say.

What is the right gift to properly thank someone for not running away, for not letting me run away? A gift certificate didn't seem right, either.

"I'm so sorry," I say. "I really did want to get you something you'd like." I start to cry.

"You're such a baby," Sam says, hugging me.

Mainly, I'm crying out of embarrassment. The coat has epaulets! What was I thinking?

"What do you say we go work on your gift, now?" Sam says.

The Test

I INTENTIONALLY WAIT until after Christmas to get my mammogram. Specifically, I wait until after Christmas—but before December 31. I've only canceled three appointments.

I wait until after Christmas because I really love Christmas. And if I have breast cancer, Christmas will be ruined. I reason that if I have breast cancer, I want to learn this after Christmas, but before New Year's. Because if I learn this before New Year's, my resolution will be to kick cancer's ass. I will have a plan. A plan equals success. If I learn this after New Year's, it will seem too late, somehow. I will sink into a deep depression and have to wait a year to start my plan of attack.

Waiting for a ghost that may never come is exhausting, and has taken more of a toll on me than I realized.

The doctor, recommended months ago by Mom's oncologist, has a way of making me feel that things are fine. More than fine. A-OK. He seems to know how fearful I am in spite of the fact that I've claimed not to be scared, says I should come to his office after I'm dressed. He wants to talk to me.

He's older than my father was. That's how I think of men now. Older than my father, or younger than my father.

"So, what are your plans?" Dr. A-OK asks.

"I'm going to get lunch, and then head back to work," I say. "On the other hand, I could have a complete mental breakdown. Do you have the results?"

"Yes. You're one hundred percent fine. But I thought now seemed like a good time to talk about your concerns," Dr. A-OK says.

"Yes, well, my mother had cancer, my grandmother had cancer—guess who's next?" I ask.

"Well, it's important to be aware of that history. It's no guarantee you'll get cancer, though. It means you're at an increased risk. Both your mother and your grandmother are still living, right? And that's good news. Even if they weren't living, I'd just encourage you to test when you're younger instead of waiting until you're thirty-eight or forty—and you've done that," he says.

"Right," I say.

"Are you planning to have children?" Dr. A-OK asks.

"Yes," I say.

"So let me lay out the options," he says.

"I have options?" I say. That had not occurred to me.

"There usually are," he says. "Depending on your level of anxiety about history repeating itself . . . you could continue with regular mammograms; have one just before you plan your pregnancy so that you won't go more than a year between tests. Continue self-exams. When you're finished having children, consider having the nodes removed," he says.

It all sounds so easy. So relaxing. He makes it sound like a nonemergency . . . I could have a facial, get my nodes removed, and then have a spa lunch.

I ask him the question to which I want the answer, but never thought I'd ask.

"When will I know that I'm safe?" I ask. "If I don't

have it at forty, am I safe, or fifty, or sixty? At what point do I relax?"

"You relax now," he says. "You don't have cancer now. All you have is an increased risk."

The conversations that I'm the most afraid to have are the ones I most need to have. They almost always come as a relief. I've danced around these questions my entire life, avoiding relief.

Nick & Toni's

WE'RE AT NICK & TONI'S sitting in the corner. We drove to East Hampton at the last minute to get here in time for dinner. It was as if we both knew we had to choose the perfect backdrop for the most important conversation we might ever have.

Sam orders what he always orders here—the elaborate pasta dish with the egg on top of it. He doesn't even look at the menu anymore. What's the point when reliable perfection has been achieved?

"I got a call from Susanna," Sam says.

"Oh," I say. "How's Chicago?"

I liked Susanna. We spoke a few times after she left Sam. The conversations were short and I had the impression she was gauging my interest in her complaints about Sam. Was she anticipating that I'd defend him? The way lawyers do? Or the way couples do? I stopped returning her calls.

"She sounds good. She said she'd heard about me and you," Sam says.

I was never really sure what to say to Sam about Susanna. They seemed really well suited until they split up. Then they seemed so obviously terribly matched I was surprised they ever got married.

"Were you in love with her when she left?" I ask.

"No," Sam says.

"Why did you stay married?" I ask.

He sits for a while.

"Honestly, it seemed easier than getting divorced," Sam says.

"Easier how?" I ask.

"I know it sounds ridiculous," Sam says. "It's not rational. I didn't want to be a divorced guy. I didn't want to move. I didn't want to decide who gets the blender or the china. We were pretty good at living separate lives together."

"I can remember driving home from the Hamptons that day, when your ankle was broken and Susanna had left," I say. "It was such a relief to me that you were in the middle of a divorce because it seemed like I might have time to figure out how to handle a relationship. Buy some how-to books, or something. It was as if I wasn't quite sure I knew how to love someone even though I'd told other men I loved them."

"I don't think I need to hear about you telling other men you love them," Sam says, smiling. "Telling me would be good enough."

"I love you," I say.

It was nearly a year of having relationships carried out in parallel with my father and Sam and my shrink. Eventually the training wheels have to come off and it's always a surprise when you find you don't need them.

Deep-Fried Pizza

I'D PLANNED AN elaborate dinner. I was going to replicate something I'd seen in the *Times* food section. Succulent duck with figs and port wine. The kind of recipe everyone longs to make but never does. I bought the ingredients. Who knew there was more than one kind of fig? But life crept in and I never quite got to it, and then I heard Sam's key in the door.

I had envisioned a scenario where he walks into the apartment, smells this great meal, and starts to believe I'm getting my act together. I'm not sure how I concocted this flawed equation.

"I didn't make dinner. . . . I told you I'd make a special dinner, and I didn't make anything," I say.

He kisses me. "Let's go out," Sam says.

I want to stay in. I've been working late interviewing receptionist candidates. Replacing one's self is no small feat. I didn't make it to the grocery store this week. I look in the freezer. Sam hangs up his coat.

"Would you eat French bread pizza?" I say. I don't mention how long it's been in the freezer.

He's in the other room still wearing his suit. He claims a suit is what he is most comfortable in, and he does seem to spend a lot of time lingering in it.

"Sure. What *is* deep-fried pizza?" Sam says.

"Deep-fried pizza?" I repeat. "I said . . . I said French bread pizza . . . but you were willing to eat deep-fried pizza? You have the absolute best attitude of anyone I've ever met."

"It's just food," Sam says.

"Deep-fried pizza is attempted murder," I say. "You're right, let's go out."

We walk to Sushi of Gari. Over sake at the crowded counter, Sam starts cleaning out his pockets. He lines his stuff up on the counter. Change. A paper clip. A mint. A ring.

"So, what do you say? Will you marry me?" Sam asks.

Congratulations

I WALK INTO Paul's waiting room and someone is in *my* seat. Slight panic. My seat is taken! There are five seats— only one is taken. The one I usually sit in. Eventually, I do sit. I sit in another seat.

I wait for Paul. He'll either open his office door and nod me in, or he'll enter through the main door, giving me pause to wonder where he's been previously. Men's room? House call? Lunch date? Slept in this morning? Once, I imagined an elaborate scenario that had him swimming laps first thing in the morning. This is the only way I could explain to myself why he would have wet hair at my ten A.M. appointment. Certainly, he didn't sleep until nine and then shower and dash to his office. He was too ideal to be late. Or to be the sort to sleep until nine.

Paul opens the door. He smiles. I stand up and walk into his office.

I go back to my favorite diversions. Arranging books on his shelf, staring at the trees outside. But the diversions don't work as well as they used to.

"I'm getting married," I say.

"Congratulations," Paul says.

"Do you think you'll ever get remarried?" I ask.

"No," Paul says.

"I knew it!" I say. "I knew you were divorced when you stopped wearing your ring and that you just didn't want to tell me."

"Once you get the bit in your mouth," Paul says.

"Okay, I'm deciding whether I should ignore the fact that you just called me a horse," I say. "Or focus on how I think you've been lying about being married."

All sorts of things are occurring to me. For the most part I'm thinking that when I get married it may be time to leave my shrink. My father's diligent understudy. Breaking up is never easy. And because it's never easy he's already slinging mud and comparing me to a horse!

"I think you might miss me if I weren't coming here anymore," I say.

"What made you think of that?" Paul asks.

"I was thinking about what being married might mean," I say. "It would probably mean leaving therapy at some point, don't you think?"

"Would it?" Paul says.

"Yes," I say. In Central Park there is a kite stuck high up in a tree. The kite looks brand new.

"I'd miss you," I say.

"What would you miss?" Paul asks.

"I don't know. The time," I say.

We sit in silence for a while.

"Yeah, it's time," Paul says.

I stand up. I'm walking toward the door.

"Again, congratulations, Emily," Paul says.

"Thanks," I say.

We sit in silence for the next thirty minutes.

Bride of Phil

WE ARE HAVING BRUNCH. Me, Mom, and Phil. They are a pair now. I'm the reason we have to wait for a table for four because we no longer fit at a deuce. There's no seeing Mom without seeing Phil. My popularity is on the decline. No more last-minute urgent phone calls about a spa day I have to attend, or a breakfast I need to be ready for in thirty minutes.

"We have some news," Mom says.

I get a pit in my stomach. One of them must have cancer again. Which one? Let it be Phil. Let it be Phil. I know, I know, that's just terrible. Please, for the love of God, let it be Phil.

"We're getting married," Phil says. "It's going to be an extravaganza."

"In three to six months," my mom says.

Phil was originally given three to six months to live. It's their magically morbid joke.

"Why wait the traditional one year?" Phil asks.

"I can't think of a single reason," I say

"It will be a momentous occasion," Phil says.

"And I know exactly what I want my dress to look like," Mom says. "I want it to be just like Tara's, but instead of white, I'd like it to be lilac. And I'll use better-quality fabrics, of course."

"Who's Tara?" I ask.

"Who's Tara?" Mom says, her eyes rolling. "Tara from *The Passionate & the Youthful*. You remember her wedding! We watched it over and over again."

"Oh, right," I say. It was a three-ring circus of a wedding. We recorded it, and even when we viewed it a second and third time, we cried at their I dos. We were so grateful for any outlet for our emotions at that time. "But you're skipping the headgear, right?"

"Undecided," Mom says.

I want to scream at the top of my lungs: What the hell do you see in each other?

I imagine Joanie shouting back: Life!

The thought of this, not her wedding, makes me eerily happy. My mom is getting married. She's leaping forward into the great unknown with a smile on her face.

"I'm thrilled for you both," I say.

"What other mother gets the double joy of planning her daughter's wedding and her own wedding?" Mom asks.

Smell of New Leather

I SMELL NEW LEATHER even before I'm inside his office, and it can mean only one thing: he got a real couch! It's brown leather. Clubby-looking. It has some strategically placed throws on it that I can't imagine him shopping for. Gifts?

"You said—"

But before he could finish, I said: "I know what I said." I lay on the couch. A deal's a deal.

There is a new painting, too. It stretched the distance of the couch, a field of poppies. Not masculine. Not feminine exactly.

"What's the story on the painting?" I ask.

"It's by a French painter. Reminded me of van Gogh without all of the craziness," Paul says.

"I think that's what people *like* about van Gogh," I say.

"Maybe," he says.

"The painting is nice. The new couch is nice. But that daybed you had? That was absurd! It wasn't good enough for you. Neither was the rug that I'm sure everyone was probably tripping over for fifteen years. So good work on getting out of your funk. I think you're starting to care about yourself again."

I hear laughter.

"What?" I say.

"I think you're going to like the couch," Paul says.

Back in the World

WENDY'S NAILS ARE painted red. First time I've seen her with a manicure—ever. Looks a little severe, but it seems so sweet that she's trying to get back into the world.

"What should I wear?" Wendy says. "I'll be going from work to a date."

"You can never go wrong with stretchy stirrup pants and an oversized T. And don't forget the scrunchie," I say. "How about a suit?"

"A suit?" Wendy asks. "My ex said that women in suits scare men. That's when I started wearing separates. I think it was too late by then."

"More casual," I agreed. "You know, Wendy, you're so organized, and on top of things, maybe relaxing your wardrobe will relax you on the date. It might be a nice complement to your strengths."

"That's good advice," Wendy says. "Thanks."

Wendy is my father's office widow. She never asked if I wanted to help clean out his office. I was surprised not to be asked about this, but grateful. My father's apartment has been organized for weeks. Wendy took his books. We donated his clothing and some of his furniture. I gave my sister his cuff links because I have to believe that there will be a time when she'll want to examine her own relationship with our father and that it will be easier for her to do so if she doesn't have to involve me.

We're almost finished with dinner, and a bottle of wine, when Wendy gets to the real reason she wanted to see me.

"I have something to ask you," Wendy says.

"Okay,"

"It's kind of awkward," Wendy says.

"Money?" I say.

"Not that awkward," Wendy says. "Well, maybe it is that awkward, but in a different way.

"I'm, um, I'm thinking of having a baby, and I have to choose a donor. A sperm donor. I keep reading the profiles of all these donors, and instead of seeming like donors they start to seem like potential dates, and it's really fogging my judgment. I just need someone to read these and tell me who's the best father on paper," Wendy says.

"That's huge. That's great," I say.

"Well, so, can you read a couple of profiles and let me know who you'd choose?" Wendy says.

Sure. Of course. I'm flattered; I'm confused.

"Why are you asking me to do this?" I ask.

"I think you're very . . . sensible. Intuitive, too," Wendy says. "By the way, if you're having a hard time choosing between two guys, look in their files and see if they have attached or detached lobes. That can be the tiebreaker. I have attached lobes, so let's vote that way," Wendy says.

Locker-Room Talk

I MEET MARJORIE at the tennis club. I stretch my legs. She walks toward me in a panic.

"I feel like jumping out a window," Marjorie says.

"Why?" I say.

She hands me a glossy piece of paper with a grainy, unidentifiable image on it.

"How many do you see?" Marjorie says.

"How many what? I don't even know what the hell I'm looking at," I say.

"Two! You see twins," Marjorie says.

"Wow—that's amazing," I say. "Congratulations. Just

think, it only took you ten months to come up with a name for one!"

"They're going to need names—shit, that didn't even occur to me," Marjorie says. "My timing is terrible. I wanted to have them two years apart."

"You get what you get—be happy about it. This year. Next year. Is there really a difference? You always wanted a big family," I say.

Marjorie wants what she didn't have when we were growing up. More kids. More noise. I want what we had before it all fell apart.

"Yeah," she says. "That's true. And I can have my boobs lifted after they're born, because I'll be all done."

"I knew you could find the silver lining," I say.

After we play tennis we go into the locker room to change. There is a naked woman drying her hair in front of an enormous mirror. She's spraying it, blowing it out, working on a genuine updo. All this—while completely naked. It's taking way too long. People are going out of their way to walk very far around her as she dries her hair.

"What's up with that?" Marjorie says.

I shrug my shoulders.

"That pubic hair is frightening. Seriously, have you ever seen so much pubic hair?" Marjorie says, more with baffled awe than judgment.

"Actually, no, I haven't. It looks like it's been grafted onto her," I say.

Marjorie starts laughing. She can't stop. "Pubic hair grafting," Marjorie says.

"Whoa, lady, tame that triangle!" I say, while throwing myself back toward the lockers, pretending the pubic hair is strangling me. The blow-dryer stopped at least fifteen seconds ago, and the woman who was drying her hair is now staring at me in disbelief.

"What are you two—twelve years old?" the woman asks.

Marjorie gathers her gear and hightails it out of the locker room.

There's no such thing as grown-up, I remember Paul saying.

The Brontë Sisters

MY REPLACEMENT STARTED today. I, Emily the intentionally incompetent, am to train the new receptionist. I am slow to dole out the nuances I've learned in my tenure here. I will pass them out like kibble.

Her name is Charlotte. She is my age approximately. I can tell from the get-go that I can teach this woman nothing. She's a highly functioning individual. Emotionally stable. Average-looking. Smart enough. Pleasant voice. Easy to laugh. She's got the whole package. Unfortunately for her, the reward for having this particular "package" is a desk job that she can keep as long as she desires. That means she'll have this job for twenty years. Perhaps not unfortunately, because she seems like she might actually enjoy answering the phone. She lifts the receiver as if performing a ballet.

"Funny, we're both named after Brontë sisters," I say.

"Do they work in the building?" Charlotte asks, while unpacking seven framed photographs of her Yorkie, Lady.

"No, they're . . . yeah. Yeah. They work in the coffee shop," I say.

I give her time to organize her dog photos and various dog statuary. She places her makeup mirror directly in front of her on the desk. Her makeup bag (yes, dogs on that, too) goes next to the mirror. In the meantime, I return to making personal calls on company time. I view this as a service to the law firm. The sooner I get on with my life, tie up the loose ends that now keep me in a state of flux, the sooner I get out the door and they move forward with a qualified receptionist. It's my last week, but if things don't work out for me on the outside, we all know I'll be back. And that won't be good for anyone.

It's taken a while, but I've worked it so most of the lawyers now answer their own phones. They grew tired of missing calls, or receiving the wrong ones. If I've taught them nothing else, they will appreciate a good receptionist. I've got high hopes for Charlotte. She moves into the job with zeal. She takes over the place. With her personal belongings on display for all to see, she's inviting people into her world. An invitation is an invitation. She's not self-conscious or embarrassed about the twisted one-dimensional canine-adoring planet from where she hails. This is self-acceptance on the grandest scale. She might be the most amazing person I've ever met.

Milestone

MY MOTHER IS STANDING on a ladder, mop in hand.

"What are you doing?" I say.

"Cleaning windows?" Mom says. "It drives me nuts to look at that dirt," Mom says.

"I'll do it," I say.

"It's okay, honey. I enjoy doing it," Mom says. "Remember the last time I did this?"

"I do," I say. "Dad helped you."

A peculiar silence follows.

"The doctor called," Mom says. "Everything is fine. One year mark. Quite a milestone."

"That's great," I say. "That's really great. And you feel good?"

"Never better," Mom says.

"Maybe the windows can wait," I say. "Besides, they already look clean."

"Phil cleaned them this morning," Mom says. "Or yesterday. He cleaned them yesterday."

"Well, was it this morning or was it yesterday?" I ask, intentionally putting her on the spot.

"Honey, listen. Since we're going to be married in a few months, Phil is moving in," Mom says.

"I'm confused. I thought he already lived here," I say.

"Oh. Okay, well I didn't know you knew that," Mom says. "I guess we can skip the pretend moving day we were planning."

Between the Lines

I'M IN THE PARKING lot of Hildreth's in East Hampton, and I'm having a phone session with Paul the shrink. It is a paved black parking lot. There are no lines to park between.

"It *is* insane," I say.

"It is insane," Paul says. "I don't understand why you didn't call me from Sam's house. He knows you're in therapy."

"Right, why do I care if he hears what I'm saying to you?" I ask.

"Yes, why do you care?" Paul asks.

"I don't know. The employees of Hildreth's are actually taking turns watching me watch them. Hold on a sec, I'm going to turn the car around so they can't see my face. They probably think I'm going to drive through the window," I say.

"Why would they think that?" Paul asks.

"Because my car is pointed toward their double glass doors, and I'm revving the engine?" I say.

It is the Friday before Valentine's Day, and Sam and I are at his place in East Hampton. Even though he says he'll take a walk while I talk to Paul, I don't quite trust the quiet house. So I insist on doing my session via phone in the car in the parking lot of a home-goods store. It's not about trusting Sam, though.

"I was half hoping you wouldn't answer," I say.

"Why?" Paul says.

"The four home pregnancy tests I've taken have all been positive. And I'm in shock," I say.

Silence.

"Nothing?" I say. "You aren't going to say anything?"

"That's wonderful. Really wonderful," Paul says. "What does Sam say?"

"Sam says 'If it's positive, why do you keep buying more tests?'" I say.

"And what else does he say?" Paul says.

"That we need to move up the wedding date," I say.

"I see," Paul says. "So you're in a parking lot with the engine running . . ."

"In case I need to make a clean break. Get away. I know what you're going to say," I say.

"What?" Paul says.

"Drive back to Sam. Experiment with what it feels like to stay when you might be tempted to run," I say.

"I don't need to say what you already know," Paul says.

Ashes

MY FATHER'S ASHES are still in the living room in an overpriced container that we bought from the undertaker. Because we were new to this death thing, we didn't know you caught a break if you bring your own container. It reminded me how, for a brief time, some supermarkets were offering a two-cent refund if you brought your old bags back.

BUT MOSTLY, IT SEEMS TO ME, it is ridiculous that you get charged for dying, for needing disposal. Is it any wonder the nation's parks and highways are littered with bodies?

The disposal, or spreading of, his ashes is sort of like cleaning out the junk drawers. Mom and I kept meaning to get to it. But there was always a good excuse not to.

Finally, in April, we scattered them in a place, two places actually, where he'd spent a lot of time. Two fistfuls of him were sprinkled in the tie department of the men's Bergdorf store. Security kept tailing us, like we were going to steal something. It was mortifying. Of course he'd said this as a joke, decades earlier, to my mother. Their joke. We figured, why not?

The rest of his ashes we poured in a wildflower garden behind our old summer house. The place we went in July and August when we were a family. There was sap on the grass from the trees, and my mother insisted that we put trash bags over our shoes before stepping on the grass. Is nothing sacred?

She and I laughed as we put Hefty bags over our shoes and paraded the urn out to the lawn. It was heavier than you'd expect. Heavier than a bag of flour.

Marjorie, Malcolm, Little Malcolm, Nana, Sam, and Phil waited in the car. Mom and I walked close to the water and an amazing old oak tree. It was a sunny, breezy day, and we lifted the lid and began pouring his ashes in increments. His ashes swirled and flew back in our face and mouth and eyes. Some settled on the grass, some flew through the air and settled on our clothing. Letting go is never easy.

ACKNOWLEDGMENTS

For being an all-around great editor, thank you, Lee Boudreaux!

For their opinons, insight, and careful reading, I appreciate the help I received from: my husband and first reader, Ed Conard, my agent, David McCormick, Leslie Falk, Gillian Linden, and Abby Holstein.

For keeping their senses of humor and being very good sports about having a writer in the family, I want to thank my mother, Jane Leader, and my sisters Linda Davis and Kelly Davis Corbett.

To Carrie Kania, Josh Marwell, Kate Pereira, Kathy Smith, Nina Olmstead, Rachel Bressler, Stephanie Linder, and Michael McKenzie of ECCO and HarperCollins, I'm amazed by your foresight and planning. Thank you!

In addition to the people mentioned above, I would be remiss in not thanking many of people who contributed to the success of my first novel, *Girls' Poker Night*: Barry

Friedberg, sister goddess Victoria Beaven Roca, Carmen Jacobson, Joan Didion, Jay McInerny, Mark O'Donnell, Adriana Trigiani, Laura Zigman, Susan Isaacs, Sandy Jones Reese, Mandy Stapf, Libby Moore, Ed Conard, David McCormick, Lee Boudreaux, Jynne Martin, and Daniel Menaker.

To the many readers who took the time to write such thoughtful letters and emails, I've been overwhelmed by your kind, heartfelt, and often very funny words.

I'd also like to thank the East Hampton Library and the New York Society Library where parts of this book were written.

A portion of the proceeds from this book are being donated to the following breast cancer organizations:

The Komen Foundation
5005 LBJ Fwy., Ste. 250
Dallas, TX 75244

National Breast Cancer Foundation
2600 Network Blvd.
Suite 300
Frisco, TX 75034

If you'd like to support the cause and make a contribution to either organization, a check can be mailed to the addresses listed above. Write ASK AGAIN LATER in the memo section of your check.

Book Club Information: If you would like the author to participate in your book club via speakerphone, please e-mail requests to *askjad@aol.com*. To download a Reading Group Guide, please visit jilldavis.com or harpercollins.com/readers.